Just a FLING

CHARITY FERRELL

Just a FLING

CHAPTER ONE

Hudson

"SAVE IT. That shit is your gig, not mine." I'm staring at my older brother, wondering when he lost his damn mind.

"You'll be doing me a huge favor," Dallas pleads.

"You want me to wash your panties? Sure. You need me to get rid of your old-school nudie mags so Lucy doesn't find out you were a little perv back in the day? I got you. *Those* are favors. What you're asking me is more than that, and you fucking know it."

"Come on. You're overreacting."

I shake my head. "I didn't withstand two tours overseas to come home and play bitch to some spoiled Hollywood princess."

I busted my ass in Marine training, slept in the shittiest conditions, and witnessed shit I'd give my left nut to un-see. No way am I moving on from that to following some high-maintenance chick around. "I've been gone for nine months, and this is the first thing you ask when I get home? Offering me some bullshit job you know I'd never take?"

"You'll be her bodyguard, not her bitch, Hudson."

"Either way, I respectively decline."

"She's not as bad as you think."

I snort.

"Do it for me. I'm going through hell right now. You taking this job will give me one less problem to worry about."

I hold up my hand. "Nuh-uh, don't you dare pull that shit."

"What shit?"

"The empathy hook you're attempting to sink into me that will make me look like a heartless bastard if I don't let you reel me in." I'd trade places with him and take his pain in a goddamn heartbeat if I could.

"Is it working?" He chuckles at my irritation. "Look, I was her security guard for five years. She's not only a damn good employer but also a friend who helped pay Lucy's medical bills and gave me paid leave to be with my family. I want to make sure she's protected, and last I heard, they haven't found anyone qualified enough to take my place. That's why I suggested you."

"How about you un-suggest me?"

He drags his hand through his shaggy brown hair. "What's your plan then, huh? The pay is better than anything here in Blue Beech. Make some fast cash, come home, and put a down payment on a house. You can quit as soon as they hire someone else."

I stay silent, and he stretches forward to punch my arm.

"You know I wouldn't ask if it wasn't important to me," he adds.

I lean back in my chair and focus on him from across his kitchen table. Dark circles ride under his sunken eyes, and stress lines that didn't exist when I left months ago stretch along his mouth. My older brother is hurting and in fear of losing the woman he loves. As his brother, it's my job to pull my shit together, put my pride aside, and help him.

His wife, Lucy's, breast cancer was caught too late and spread too fast. The doctors aren't sure how much time she has left. She's only thirty-one, and her diagnosis was a shock to us. Dallas quit his job as head security guard for Stella Mendes and returned home to be there for her.

"Fine," I groan, holding up a finger. "I'll do it but on one condition."

He raises a brow.

"It's only temporary. Two months max, so you tell them to get their asses on finding a replacement."

He blows out a ragged breath. "Thank you. Your flight leaves in the morning."

"The hell? You already booked my flight?"

He nods.

"What if I'd said no?"

"I'd have Lucy ask you."

"You play fucking dirty." It's one thing to argue with him, but no way can I say no to Lucy.

"This job will also get you out of town so shit can cool down for a minute. It's a win-win."

"I don't need shit to cool down." My muscles tense while I hold in my rage—the topic pissing me off more than the job offer.

He gives me a stern look. "Don't do something you'll regret."

"We're not having this conversation." I pinch the bridge of my nose. "It's off-limits right now, you hear me?"

"I understand, brother. I'd be one furious motherfucker, too."

THERE'S no missing the curious stares following me when I walk into the Down Home Pub, the hot spot in town if you're craving a beer, good time, or want to drown your sorrows.

Dallas forced me to go out for drinks—a pick-me-up for us both was what he called it. My dumb ass should've known it was more than grabbing a quick beer and shooting the shit.

A blue *Welcome Home Hudson* banner hangs at the front of the bar, and the pub is packed with familiar faces—people I've known all my life. Months ago, I would've loved this surprise.

Now? Not so much.

I've lived in Blue Beech, Iowa, all my life. It's a small town where everyone knows everyone's business. People say that about all small towns, but Blue Beech is the real deal. Everyone knew my fiancé was fucking around on me and planning a wedding with my best friend *on our scheduled wedding date* before I did. News doesn't travel as fast as word of mouth when you're overseas with limited communication.

Cameron sent me a bullshit Dear John letter. Every word was a stab to the gut. I ripped it up and burned the pieces. Crumbling relationships and marriages are a regular occurrence in military life. I'd become just another statistic.

Dallas hands me a beer, and I smile before chugging it in one go—savoring the bitter yet delicious malted barley. I slap my hand onto the bar and ask the bartender, Maliki, to pour us another round.

There's no missing the pity stares shooting in my direction, confirming everyone knows about Cameron. I spot a group of guys I played football with in high school huddled around the table and stroll in their direction. When I'm almost there, someone sticks their foot out in an attempt to trip me.

They fail, but I'm pissed.

What the fuck?

I turn around, ready to take my anger out on the jackass, but that outrage dissipates when I see her.

"Well, if it isn't the biggest asshat in the world. Sorry I'm late, but the hospital has been a madhouse," Lauren, my younger sister, says.

I laugh when she attempts to wrap her short arms around me in a hug and pat her on the head when she pulls away. "No biggie. I've only been here a few minutes."

She grins. "I've missed you. Guys aren't as scared to mess

with me when you're gone. I've had to resort to my pepper spray and AK-47."

"You don't own an AK-47."

"True, but doesn't it sound badass when I say I do? You should probably buy me one for my birthday."

"I'm never buying you a gun. Hell, I wouldn't put it past you to shoot some poor bastard who said the wrong thing to you."

She laughs. "You know the tempers of the Barnes family aren't one to be reckoned with."

I debated on going home, but Blue Beech is all I've ever known. As I sit down and enjoy another beer, I'm happy I agreed to come instead of drinking my sorrows away in Dallas's basement.

That happiness lasts only twenty minutes and two beers in. I'm beginning to relax while Lauren divulges her latest dating fail when she stops mid-conversation and slams her drink down.

"I cannot believe that son of a bitch and hussy would show their faces here," she yells.

I look away from her fuming face to see what has her attention.

"Everyone in this godforsaken town knows your party is here tonight," she spats.

My hands turn numb, and I nearly drop my beer while the taste of bile swims up my throat.

The bar goes silent.

Even the jukebox cuts off for the ensuing shitshow.

I shift in my seat in an attempt to cool the fury crackling through me like a lit match.

There she is.

Cameron Pine.

The woman who decided I wasn't worth the wait is heading straight in my direction with the asshole she left me for at her side.

She's wearing a denim skirt and the same flannel top she wore the night I proposed. Her face is void of emotion, her curly blond hair swept back into a ponytail, and she's sporting her cherry red lipstick—a color she'd stained my dick with countless times. I used to love it when she marked me. She might've fucked me over, but that doesn't stop me from thinking she's breathtakingly gorgeous.

My gaze moves from her to something not so beautiful. A sight so fucking rancid it makes my stomach churn. Grady was my best friend who took my asking to watch over her too literal. I wanted him to make sure she was safe, not keep her pussy warm for me.

"Cameron better not come over here, or I will find an AK-47 and run her ass out of this bar," Lauren says.

My sister is loyal to a fault. Cameron was her best friend, but she burned all ties and threatened to kick her ass on multiple occasions when she found out about the affair. Even now, I'm not sure my baby sis will keep her cool and not choke slam Cameron *and* Grady.

"I had no idea they were coming," Dallas says, rushing to our table. He went outside ten minutes ago to call Lucy and check on her. "They obviously weren't invited."

"Unless I plan on moving out of Blue Beech forever, I'm bound to run into them," I reply. "Cameron wasn't happy with me and chose to be with someone who could be that nine-to-five, at the dinner table every night husband. I'm not that man."

The problem is, I still can't bring myself to hate Cameron.

Although, I'm fucking livid with Grady.

It takes two people to have an affair, I'm well aware, and it's wrong for me to place all the blame on him, but I can't put it on the woman I loved for over a decade.

The bar stays silent while everyone watches them grow closer.

"Hudson," Grady says when he reaches us. He looks stressed, scared, and I can't blame him. "Can we talk?"

Cameron stands behind him and rests her hand on his shoulder.

"You need to leave, asshole," Lauren demands. "And take that cheating skank with you."

"My sister is right," Dallas says. "You two have some nerve showing up here. Let's not make this uglier than necessary."

I hold up my hand to stop my siblings from going on. "It's cool." My eyes narrow in on Grady, and I can tell it wasn't his idea to come. "I'd love to have a chat and hear your pathetic ass excuse for stabbing me in the back over a goddamn chick." I tilt my head toward the back door, grab my beer, and he follows me to the exit.

I snatch his shirt collar and slam him against the brick exterior as soon as the door shuts behind us. "I told you to watch out for her, not fuck her!"

His lower lip trembles when I wrap my hand around his neck. "I'm sorry. I'm so fucking sorry, Hudson. It just happened!"

I tighten my hold on him and inch closer until we're nose to nose. "Having sex with someone doesn't *just happen*. You had time to stop. You could've walked away. Hell, not only did you fuck her behind my back but you also proposed to her while she was wearing my engagement ring. That sure as fuck doesn't *just happen*!"

It takes every bit of restraint in me not to smash my fist in his face. Cameron is vain enough that she would dump his ass if he weren't a pretty boy any longer.

Maybe I should.

"I love her, Hudson," he chokes out.

His words add fuel to my burning fire, and he grunts when I pull him closer, only to slam him back against the wall.

"She was mine!" I scream.

I release him and take a step back at the sound of the back door opening. Cameron steps out, and I hold my breath with a snarl. We haven't talked in months. I never replied to her pathetic letter. She said enough for the both of us.

My skin crawls as the memories of us and the plans we

made for when I got home smack into me. She was supposed to be my wife, the mother of my children, and the woman I grew old with.

"Don't … don't do this, Hudson," she begs. "We came here to do the right thing and clear the air." Her voice lowers. "I'm sorry for hurting you. We both are."

I'm a tough guy who has withstood a lot of shit, but fighting back this hurt of betrayal from two people I trusted with my life kills me. Words neglect me while I stare into her baby blue eyes. It's not as easy to push my anger out on her like it is with Grady.

Tears fall down her cheeks. "He was there for me when you weren't. I begged you not to leave me again and told you how difficult it was being alone. I wanted a family, but you didn't care!"

"It was my fucking job, Cameron!" I scream.

"You're right, and the job of being a military wife isn't for me. I'm sorry."

"It is what it is," I mutter. "Stay the hell away from me. You deserve each other."

I turn around and walk away without another glance at them.

A few months away from this town might be what I need to clear my head and get my shit straight.

Let's only hope this chick is easy to deal with.

CHAPTER TWO

Hudson

I DEPART from the terminal after landing at LAX and stroll through the mob of people rushing around with phones in their hands. I'm not a fan of crowds. Solitude is more my thing, but I have a feeling I better get used to the contrary. Dallas has told me stories about working for Stella. Fans and paparazzi follow her around like a shadow.

Instead of going back to my party last night, I headed to Dallas's place and watched Disney movies with my niece, Maven.

I went from the plan of coming home to fuck my fiancé senseless to sitting on the couch with my niece watching a cartoon about a nitwit teen who traded her voice for legs in order to get laid by Prince Charming. Sleep wasn't my friend, and the cherry on top of my time home was Dallas waking me up at the ass crack of dawn to drive me to the airport.

I snag my luggage and sweep my gaze over the room. Dallas texted me directions of what to do when I landed. Stella's driver will be here to give me a ride to her place. I scan the signs being held up by people, waiting until I see the one with my name on it, and make my way over to the gray-haired man wearing a suit.

"You Jim?" I ask him.

He nods. "You Hudson?"

"Sure am."

I shake his hand and stop him from grabbing my luggage before he leads me out of the airport to a black SUV with windows tinted so dark they have to be illegal. I toss my bag in the back seat and sit in the front.

"Have you worked for Stella long?" I ask when he starts the car and leaves the parking garage.

Traffic is bumper-to-bumper.

Why would anyone want to live in this shit?

"Almost five years," Jim answers. "She hired me after your brother started, but unlike her bodyguards, I don't travel with her. I only drive when she's in LA." He glances over at me with pain on his face. "Dallas was damn good at his job, and I hope you're the same. I also hate to bring this up, but I'm sorry for what's happened to Lucy. I lost my wife to cancer last year and can't imagine the pain of losing her so young."

"Thank you, and I'm sorry for your loss. My sister-in-law is as tough as nails. She'll make it through this stronger than ever."

That's what I tell myself. My family is trying our best to stay positive.

I make small talk with Jim for the rest of the ride, and he punches in the passcode after we stop in front of a security gate. I stare at the lavish Spanish-style home in awe as he drives up to it. Homes in Blue Beech are nothing like this. Cameron and I rented a two-bedroom farmhouse that looked like a shack compared to this place.

"Hot damn," I mutter. "Some crib for a twenty-five-year-old."

Jim parks and cuts the ignition. "Working on a long-standing, Emmy-award-winning TV show gives you a pretty decent paycheck."

"I'd say so." It's too excessive for one person, in my opinion. "Does she live here alone?"

He nods. “Her sister stayed with her for a while but moved to New York six months ago.”

The scent of vanilla hits me when I walk through the front door, and I take a look around, admiring the hardwood floors and cathedral ceilings before making it to the living room. A massive stone fireplace is the highlight of the room until you look through the floor-to-ceiling windows that give one of the most remarkable views I’ve ever seen.

I understand now why she bought the place.

That fucking view.

I could sit out there and think for hours.

My attention moves from the outside when two women walk into the room. Their mouths drop when they notice me, and I rudely stare as they come closer.

I recognize Stella immediately.

How could I not?

Stories and images of her are plastered on every magazine cover in grocery store checkout lanes, and she stays on TV with endless reruns. Cameron used to make me watch those stupid award shows with her, and Stella was a consistent winner.

Even with all that, I never expected her to be this beautiful. I can’t take my eyes off her full-figured body. She’s enthralling, flawless, fucking perfection. No wonder every cameraman wants a shot of her.

Stella Mendes is a woman who can bring a man to his knees with the slightest hint of a smile. Hell, she doesn’t even have to smile. Just her presence makes you hungry for more.

Her straight hair, the color of coal, flows down her shoulders, framing her heart-shaped face with minimal makeup. Skintight white jeans show off her curves and stop a few inches from her ankles, and a black silk tank hangs loose on her shoulders, giving me a glimpse of her honey-colored skin.

Fuck me.

Good thing I’m only here until they find someone to take over the job.

Her attractiveness doesn't change my opinion of her. She might be gorgeous, but that doesn't mean she's a decent person. Cameron has told me stories about Stella being a spoiled diva who expects people to jump when she yells. There were times it was difficult for Dallas to come home for the holidays because of her hectic schedule.

That shit won't fly with me.

I'll work for her but won't be ordered around like a dog.

Stella holds out her hand to me. "Hudson, thank you for coming." Her voice is flat, and I can't tell if she's impartial or pissed that I'm here.

I shake her hand. It feels soft against my calloused skin. "No problem."

She jerks her head toward the petite redhead at her side that looks around the same age as her. "This is my assistant, Willow."

Willow smiles and gives me a friendly wave before clapping her hands. "Now that the introductions are out of the way, we have so much to do. You two will be spending a lot of time together, so I want to make sure you take care of my girl, Hudson."

Stella flinches at her remark and looks like she'd rather kick me out of her house.

Feeling is mutual, sweetheart.

CHAPTER THREE

Stella

OH FUCK.

Not good. Not good.

I'm so screwed.

My new bodyguard is …

I can't even think of the right words to describe him.

Mouthwatering?

I laugh to myself.

I can't come up with something more original and less lame than that?

Sexy. Masculine. Dominating.

Unfortunately, all humans with a penis are off-limits to me right now.

Hudson is built, muscles aplenty, but not like the men who spend forty hours a week lifting weights at the gym to score the perfect six-pack for their next Instagram post. He gives off a tough demeanor effortlessly.

Someone would be batshit crazy to mess with him, and that's exactly what I look for in a bodyguard. His ash-brown hair is short in the front and buzzed on the sides in your typical military cut. He didn't dress up for the occasion—wearing a pair of old jeans complete with worn holes, a white tee, and beat-up boots.

Even though we barely know each other, I already feel safe with him.

The downside to him being here is that I'm certain he's not my biggest fan. The grimace on his face made it clear he'd rather be anywhere but here.

Dallas has told me plenty about Hudson over the years. He's a small-town guy who spent the past eight years serving our country. He isn't into the whole Hollywood buzz and has called his brother a dumbass countless times for working for me.

He had to be desperate to take the job.

We say goodbye to Jim and head into my office. I get straight to business as soon as we sit down.

"Willow will keep you updated on my schedule," I tell him.

As if on cue, Willow hands him a folder and starts rambling off instructions. "Everything you need to know is in here, including all contact numbers, addresses, and emails. There's also a blueprint of the house, details of each stop during Stella's press tour, and a map of every hotel she's staying in."

Hudson listens and nods.

"How long have you been in the bodyguard business?" Willow asks. "Dallas didn't list any references other than the fact that you're his brother, and that's all that mattered."

He scratches his head, and his voice is rough when he answers. "This is my first bodyguard job."

"What?" Willow yells, looking at me in shock.

I expected her reaction, which is why I didn't tell her. I trust Dallas's word.

"So … you've never worked in this field *at all*?" Willow asks him.

I suck in a breath when he leans forward, plants his elbows on the table, and doesn't look fazed as he stares at Willow.

"I've never worked as a bodyguard, but I have plenty of experience fighting for my country, providing security at embassies, and putting my life on the line daily for the safety of others. That should be enough training for this job, don't you think? I pay attention to every movement around me, and my mind is always on the job. *Always*. And if it makes you feel better, I'm only here until you find a *more qualified* replacement."

We both stare at him, stunned and speechless.

Holy fucking hotness.

That's a damn good answer.

"HE'S CUTE," Willow says when we're alone in my bedroom.

We showed Hudson his room and left him to unpack his bag … and hopefully take a happy pill to get out of his cranky mood.

She holds up a finger. "Correction. He's not cute. *Cute* is how you describe a three-year-old freckled kid. That guy is a whole lot of man hotness. *All man* hotness."

Willow isn't just my assistant. She's also my best friend. I can count on her more than anyone. She always has my back and won't bullshit me when I'm being stupid. Frankly, she doesn't kiss my ass like most people.

I narrow my eyes at her. "Don't go there."

"It's time to move on from that douchebag."

"I *have* moved on from Knox. When I found out he bought a house and moved that pink-haired chick in, it was my reality check. He and I knew we weren't meant to be, but we were too comfortable with each other to cut the cord. He isn't the reason I'm saying don't go there. My situation is. I can't mess around with my security guard. You know mixing business with pleasure is a big no-no in my book. Not to mention, the dude looks like he can't even stand the sight of me."

She climbs onto my bed and sits across from me. "Yeah, I'm not sure what's up his ass, but maybe he'll warm up to you. And hey, just because he works for you doesn't mean you can't have a little fun." She wiggles her shoulders back and forth. "You need to get laid before cobwebs start growing down there. Lack of dick is also making you very irritable. Get some dick. Grow a smile. Just like he said he does his job, I'm sure he gives one hundred percent in the bedroom."

I throw my head back to stop myself from laughing. "Why am I friends with you again?"

"Because I'm Team Get Stella Laid."

"Don't get your hopes up. Last I heard from Dallas, Hudson is engaged to some longtime girlfriend. Guys meet their wives in like the third grade in their hometown."

She frowns. "Well, if you can't get a piece of him, we need to find you someone else."

"Reality check. Getting laid in my situation is not only doubtful but stupid."

She gives me an annoyed glare. "You can bitch about it all you want, but I don't feel sorry for you. I told you not to do it."

We've gone round and round about this.

"It was the best move for my future. My career trumps relationships and sex. I won't walk through my door one night and find my career sticking his cock into another chick."

She rolls her eyes. "Oh please, you'll always have work. You've had constant work for years because you're damn talented. Don't let them assholes tell you otherwise."

"It's a big deal migrating from television to movies. I want people to take me seriously and stop seeing me as only Clementine."

Clementine Storms was the character I played on my show. She was a geeky girl who found out she was a witch and spent her time experimenting and fucking up every spell and potion she tried.

She snorts. "People aren't going to take you seriously if word gets out about what you're doing. You'll be the joke of showbiz. They'll sever all respect, resulting in you becoming desperate and taking bad roles on the Lifetime channel where your husband plots to kill you."

I scowl. "I'll take my chances."

She's right. My credibility will be demolished, which was why I refused at first, but eventually, they broke me down. It was the best for my career is what they insisted. I question myself daily on whether I made the right decision.

"CAN I ASK YOU SOMETHING?" Hudson asks.

Willow left twenty minutes ago, so it's only the two of us. I hoped maybe he'd lighten up, but so far, all he's giving me is the cold shoulder. Hudson is more intense than his brother. I immediately felt comfortable with Dallas. He cracked a few jokes, told me stories about his family, and was an open book. Hudson is distant, glowering, and humorless.

"Shoot," I answer. It's about damn time he seemed interested in something.

He runs his hand through his hair. "I should've asked this earlier." He pauses and looks around. "What exactly are my duties here? What do I do all day?"

"Like Willow said, be prepared to spend time with me, *a lot* of time with me. You travel with me and stay here when I'm home."

His face shifts into a more guarded expression with my last statement. Dallas must have failed to inform him that tidbit of information.

I shrug. "I like to feel safe."

"I'll do my best to keep you that way." He leans against the doorframe and crosses his arms. "Have you ever had any situations?"

"Stalker wise?"

He nods.

"A few, but most of them were with my old bodyguard. It

became less frequent after I hired your brother. He did a good job scaring off the creeps, so they never got close enough to cause me any harm."

I'm not sure how much Dallas told him about the responsibilities of this job. I've been stalked, harassed, and sent death threats. I do what I love, but that doesn't mean it doesn't come with risks.

CHAPTER FOUR

Hudson

"WHAT THE FUCK, DALLAS?" I ask as soon as he answers my call. "I'm living with this chick?"

I want to shove my foot up his ass. It was stupid for me not to ask more questions before hopping on a plane to take an unknown job.

Dallas chuckles. "I see you made it safe and sound. How was your flight?"

"Shitty. I gave away my first-class ticket to some pregnant gal who needed it more than I did. Now answer my question. What the fuck did you get me into?" I figured I'd be crashing at a hotel, not her house.

"Of course, you stay there. That's what I did when Lucy moved back home."

The only reason Dallas moved to LA and took the bodyguard job was because Lucy wanted to spread her wings and get a taste of life outside Blue Beech. The big city wasn't what she imagined, so she moved home after getting pregnant with Maven. Somehow, she and Dallas managed to keep a healthy long-distance relationship while he stayed in LA.

"Lucy was cool with that?" I ask.

"I hope you're not insinuating what I think you are. I'm a

married man who has the love of his life. There's no need for another woman. My relationship with Stella was strictly professional."

"How beautiful," I mutter.

"I got you a kick-ass job with great pay. A thank you would be nice."

"Thanks," I grumble. "What exactly am I supposed to do here? Hang out with this chick all day and night? I'll go fucking nuts."

"It's not all day and night. If you need time off, ask her. You'll be spending the next week attending promotional events and screenings for her new movie. Your lucky ass gets to travel and stay in the nicest hotels for free. Quit bitching and enjoy it."

"Do I have to paint her nails and braid her hair, too?"

"If you're into that shit, go ahead. She might not be too keen on your offer. This might surprise you, but she's a pretty private person."

I scoff. *Yeah right.* If you make the decision to be famous, you're choosing to give your privacy up and giving consent to all your dirty laundry being aired out to the world.

"What did you do with her?" I ask.

Dallas is more of a people person than I am. Maybe he'll have some decent ideas to get me through this.

"We watched movies. I read. Find something you have in common."

"We have nothing in common."

"Stay optimistic. You never know."

He changes the subject by giving me an update on Lucy. We talk for a good hour before I hang up to get ready for bed. It's after eleven, and I'm nowhere near tired, but I don't know what else to do with myself.

My bedroom is on the main floor in what I assume is the in-law suite. It includes a bathroom, a full kitchenette, and a desk filled with monitors giving me a view from every camera on the property.

I undress, turn on the TV, and slide into the world's most comfortable bed. My next three hours are spent tossing and turning until I get annoyed enough to go to my bag for an Ambien.

I go to the kitchenette for a glass, but the cabinet I open is empty.

I check another one.

Empty again.

I crack open the door and tiptoe down the dark hallway toward the kitchen. I make it around the corner at the same time a light flips on, and I collide with something … or *someone.*

"Fuck!" a high-pitch voice shouts.

I stumble back to find Stella standing in front of me with her hand settled on her chest as she takes deep breaths.

"You scared the living shit out of me," she says between pants.

It looks bad, but I can't stop myself from sweeping my gaze down her body and appreciating the view she's giving me. My dick is enjoying it as well. Purple silk shorts small enough to be considered panties stop at the base of her thighs. A matching tank stops above her belly button, showing off her tan hips and belly button ring.

Stella has curves for days that I could explore for even longer. Every trace of makeup is gone from her face. Her hair is in a messy ponytail at the top of her head, a few tendrils sweeping in front of her wide eyes.

It's my first day on the job, and she's already trying to kill me.

"Shit," I finally stutter out. "I'm sorry. I thought you'd be asleep."

She's still startled but waves off my apology. "No biggie." She always seems to be on edge—like she's waiting for a killer to barge through the door with a chainsaw.

The room falls silent, and I start getting uncomfortable when her eyes drop down my body, not going any further than my cock. Her head tilts to the side as if she's studying my junk, and I don't understand why until I glance down.

I'm only wearing boxer briefs, and they're not regular boxer briefs.

It's the pair Dallas had given me as a gag gift.

Written across my cock are the words: *Take Me To Your Beaver.*

I clear my throat, and it takes a second to gain her attention. She's smirking when she finally looks at me.

"Take me to your beaver?" she asks, laughing. "*Nice,* and here I thought you had no sense of humor. Only on your underwear does your personality come out."

"They were a gag gift from my dickhead brother. I didn't get the chance to go through my clothes when I got home, so I threw random shit in my suitcase."

That's a lie.

The truth is, Cameron packed up my belongings while I was gone and dropped them off at Dallas's place when she moved Grady in. She conveniently forgot to also drop off the furniture, appliances, and electronics I bought.

She smiles. "Can't say I can complain about them."

My dick stirs. I need to reroute this conversation before I end up taking my cock to her beaver.

"There are no glasses in the cabinet," I say.

"The kitchen is always open. I'm pretty sure Dallas never used that kitchenette." She turns to flip on another light, and the kitchen lights up like the Vegas Strip. "Can't sleep?"

I shake my head.

"Me either. I'm putting on some tea. Want a cup?"

"The only kind of tea I drink is laced with sugar and served on ice. Not sure that'll exactly make me tired."

She grabs a teapot, fills it with water, and sets it on the stove. "It's herbal tea. Chamomile. My insomnia remedy."

We're standing in her kitchen both damn near naked, and she's offering me a cup of tea.

Can this get any more awkward?

I might as well make the best of the situation. She's not freaking out or rushing away in embarrassment, and I'll look like a dipshit if I do.

I shrug and sit down on a barstool. "It's worth a shot. Why can't you sleep?"

"I have a lot on my mind."

I raise a questioning brow, a silent plea to continue, and am surprised when she does.

"I'm making a significant career change. This is my first big role in a movie, and I want people to like it … to like me. This is my chance to prove that I can do more than play some teenage witch."

"Do you like it?"

She nods.

"That's all that matters then." I throw my arms out to gesture to the kitchen. "You must have decent talent, considering you're able to afford a home like this at your age."

"Money doesn't equal talent."

"Good point."

"Do you not like me?"

The bluntness of her question surprises me. *Shit.* This isn't the conversation I want to have with her.

"What do you mean?" I ask, playing dumb.

"You have this wall up, and it seems you'd rather be anywhere but here. I mean, I'm not expecting you to be my biggest fan, but it's like I ruined your childhood Christmas or something."

"You want me to be honest?"

"I wouldn't have asked you if I didn't."

"I'm sure it comes as no surprise that I didn't want to take this job."

"Why? Because you think I'm a terrible person?"

"Never said that."

She leans against the counter and crosses her arms. "Actions speak louder than words, homeboy."

"I don't know you."

"Exactly, so you have no right to judge me so early."

"*But,*" I stress. "I've heard stories."

She snorts. "Didn't think you were one of those dudes. Stories from where?"

"Not from my brother," I rush out. I want to make that clear. Dallas has never said a bad word about Stella and has always kept her business private. "From magazines and shit." *And Cameron.*

She rolls her eyes. "Magazines and shit? Those are some credible sources, let me tell ya." She grins arrogantly. "It's okay. You don't have to like me. Not everyone has good taste."

Damn. Maybe she does have some spark in her.

I love me a smart-ass woman.

"Trust me, I have good taste," I correct. "And a good eye for character. So far, you haven't done anything too diva-like, but we've only known each other for a few hours. No one shows their flaws and bad side this early."

She stares at me blankly. "Does that mean you're hiding your flaws from me? You have some demon hidden away in there? Are you a psychopath or one of those men who like to be dressed up in a diaper and then changed as sexual foreplay?"

I can't stop a smile from flashing over my lips.

Spunk, yeah, she has it.

"The last two are a huge ass negative." *Internal demons? Possibly.* My stomach knots. "I'm sure you'll find qualities I have that you don't like. No one is perfect."

This conversation is taking a huge turn from where I wanted it to go. My plan was to drink this so-called miraculous sleep tea, have limited conversation, and get my ass some sleep.

"Have you ever watched my show?" she asks.

"Can't say I have. I tend to be an action more than teen witch fan."

Maven asked me countless times to watch Stella's show with her, but I was never interested. A hint of sadness stretches over

Stella's face, and she turns around when the teapot whistles through our tension. Grabbing two tea packets, she places them in the mugs before pouring in the water.

"So … why can't you sleep," is her next question.

I scrub a hand over my face. "It's only my second night back in the States. It usually takes time to adjust to the different time zone."

She hands me a pink mug. "Where were you stationed?"

"Afghanistan, both times."

"Do you think you'll go back?"

"I promised my family I wouldn't, but I'm not sure now." There's nothing to keep me here now. The tea scorches the tip of my tongue when I take a drink. It's too bland for my taste but not terrible.

She puckers her full lips and blows into her cup. "Why aren't you sure?"

"Shit has changed. People changed. I changed. My situation is different than when I made that promise."

"I say do whatever makes you happy." She grins and holds up her cup when I yawn. "Told you it works." She slides across the kitchen floor in her socks. "Good night, Hudson. Hopefully, you'll like me tomorrow because we have a long day ahead of us."

I turn around in my chair to look at her. "What do you mean?"

"We're flying out in the morning to finish off the promotional tour. Didn't Dallas tell you?"

I shake my head. "Nope. Must've slipped his mind."

"Now you know. Get some rest."

I give her a small smile. "Good night, Stella."

I turn off the kitchen lights and take the tea with me to my room. Even though I'm growing drowsy, something is irritating me. I grab my laptop from its sleeve and open iTunes. When I find her show, I buy every season and make it through the first two episodes before dozing off.

CHAPTER FIVE

Stella

"YOU READY TO GET THIS party started?" Willow asks when she strolls into my bedroom.

Her red hair is pulled back in two tight French braids, and she's wearing a bright green maxi dress. Like me, Willow likes to travel comfortably.

I'm sitting on my bed in a similar dress, except mine is black, and double-checking I have my passport and everything I need for the trip.

"By the way," Willow goes on. "I saw your hot bodyguard downstairs in the kitchen making coffee. Someone needs to pull the stick from his ass."

I'm about to tell her about our conversation last night but stop myself. She'll only try to push him between my legs more.

"He's probably just tired," I say, suddenly feeling the need to defend him. "He's only been home a few days and is still adjusting to the time difference."

She grins and sits down across from me. "Dang, look at you Ms. Know-It-All. Did he tell you that?" Her face scrunches up when I nod. "I bet his girlfriend wasn't happy about him leaving to come here after only being home a few days."

"I think they broke up."

"Did your new bestie disclose that as well?"

"No, but he said he promised his family he wouldn't deploy again, but shit has changed now."

"Hmm … it sounds like both of you are in need of releasing some tension. You know what helps with that?"

"A massage? Oreo cookies?"

"A *massage* to your clitoris. Oreo cookies licked off your body."

I shove her arm. "Um, gross. You know I'd freak out if crumbs got in my bed."

She sighs. "One of these days, I'm going to find you a good man."

I sigh back more dramatically. "One of these days, I'm going to find you a good man, so you stay out of my love life."

Willow has a boyfriend, and he's not my biggest fan. Nor am I his. The guy is a loser, but she loves him, so all I can do is support her. That doesn't mean I always hold myself back from throwing jabs about him now and then. She can do so much better than a man she's caught cheating and sending dick pics to other women.

"If you don't start dating, you'll be eighty, wrinkly, and living alone with your sixty-something cats drinking whiskey and whining about how much men suck."

"As long as there's alcohol involved, it sounds like a promising future. Whiskey and pussies."

She rolls her eyes, jumps off my bed, and slaps my leg to do the same. "Until then, we have a plane to catch. Your luggage was brought downstairs by Muscled Marine, so as soon as you're ready, we can leave."

"Muscled Marine? You need Jesus."

"And you need some dick to get a better sense of humor."

Hudson is still in the kitchen when we make it downstairs. He's dressed this time, which makes me frown that I won't be getting another view of his finely sculpted chest that runs down to washboard abs.

Even with my tea, I didn't sleep well last night. I couldn't stop thinking about him being downstairs. I mentally made a list of questions to ask him and thought of different ways to show him I'm not who he thinks I am.

"Good morning, ladies," he says when he notices us and holds up a cup. "Coffee?"

"Dear God, yes," I say around a yawn. "Coffee before talkie." Coffee is my liquid heroin. I'm a caffeine aficionado.

Hudson chuckles. His laughter is what I expected it to be—deep, like it's coming from the pit of his stomach and forcing its way up his throat.

He pours me a cup and slides it across the island to me. "Coffee … because crack is bad for you."

"I took the road less traveled … that led to Starbucks, and that's made all the difference," I reply with a smile.

He looks impressed at my comeback. "Want to hear a joke? Decaf."

"Coffee, a liquid hug for your brain."

Oh my god.

Are we flirting?

Are we having a moment?

Over coffee puns?

Are we really flirting in this ridiculously lame way?

Our eyes are locked, his dark gaze impaling mine, and his mouth curves into a bigger grin. If it takes coffee and a lame joke to get him to crack a smile, I'll take it.

"I feel like I'm interrupting a moment," Willow says. "A coffee flirting I don't know what the hell is going on moment." She gestures back and forth between Hudson and me. "That's why I don't drink that shit. It makes people all weird and fidgety."

Hudson laughs while breaking eye contact with me. "It's a

non-coffee drinker thing, Willow. You think we're crazy when it's really you."

And our moment has been shot down.

Thanks, best friend.

"Whatever," Willow mutters. "We have a plane to catch. Ready to go?"

Hudson finishes his coffee, rinses out his cup, and places it in the dishwasher. "I'm ready for whatever I'm getting myself into."

"I promise it's nothing as crazy as jumping out of planes and all of that other dangerous shit you did with your last job," Willow comments.

"I enjoy jumping out of planes. There's nothing that compares to that rush," Hudson fires back.

"No thank you on that," I cut in. "If God wanted me to fly, he would've given me wings."

"Correct me if I'm wrong, but we're about to board a plane that *flies*," he counters.

"Big difference."

"Yeah, your choice isn't nearly as fun."

"Maybe I'll have to try it sometime then."

I'm totally lying. This girl is not going to be hanging out in the air solo anytime soon, but I do want him to change his mind about me, to see that I'm not some spoiled diva who only eats pink Starbursts and makes my assistant go through bags of them to pick out all the other colors. Although, I do wish that rumor was true. Pink is the best flavor. Unfortunately, Willow would quit in a second if I told her to do something like that.

That's why my ex, Knox, and I connected so well. He knew this life and understood not to believe everything written in the headlines.

Real stories don't sell. Scandals do. Relationship rumors do.

Willow shoves my side in excitement and is practically jumping up and down when Hudson leaves the kitchen to grab his bag.

"I love being right," she squeals. "He totally has a thing for you. Fingers crossed he's single."

I give her a dirty look when she points at my vagina.

"I hope you waxed that kitty of yours."

CHAPTER SIX

Hudson

A GUY FALLS down in the seat across from me and stretches out his hand. "What's up, man? I'm Josh."

He's a built dude, a few inches shorter than me, and looks like he spends ample time at the gym. My money is on him being a boxer or a guy into MMA. His blond hair is tightly combed back into a man-bun.

I lean forward to shake it. "Hudson."

"You Stella's new bodyguard?"

I nod.

"I'm Eli's."

Eli is Stella's co-star and love interest in her new movie. During our drive to the airport, Willow filled me in on the cast, the movie title, and what we'll be doing.

"You have any tips for me?" I ask.

My brother's advice was to watch out for assholes and to always have Stella's back. She's had a few scary run-ins where Dallas had to tackle people to the ground. One guy even tried sticking a camera up her skirt. *Fucking creeps.*

"It's a decent gig if you don't work for an asshole," Josh says. "Eli isn't bad, and from what I've seen so far, Stella seems to be cool." He throws his arm out to gesture to the private plane we're on. "Another perk is the travel. There's no way I'd be living life like this if it weren't for my job." He pauses as a smile passes over his face. "And let's not forget about the ladies. It's a pussy magnet. Women sleep with me, hoping it'll bring them closer to whatever dude I'm working for. Although it might not be as easy for you since you're working for a chick."

"Yeah, I don't think women will be busting down doors to sleep with me thinking it might lead them into Stella's panties, and I'm not one to judge, but I don't bat for the other team."

"We'll be spending some time together, so if I have any extras, I'll send them your way."

Josh winks like his *favor* is equivalent to giving me a kidney or some shit.

My attention moves away from him when Willow moves past us in the aisle. She stops and turns around to look at us.

"Extras?" she repeats while giving Josh a cold glare. Her attention then moves to me. "Don't let this idiot corrupt you, Hudson. He's a bad influence."

"Ignore her," Josh argues. "Willow thinks I have cooties."

Willow stares at him in a look that resembles disgust. "Correction, I believe you have the adult version of cooties: STDs." She gives him a final snarl before leaving us and sitting by Stella in the row behind Josh.

Josh laughs, not realizing she's making fun of him and not flirting. "I've been trying to hit that for a while now."

"I take it you're failing?" I ask. *Of course, he is.*

"She's not giving it up, but I'll break her down soon. I'm sure of it."

"Good luck."

Willow seems cool so far. Josh … not so much. I hope she doesn't fall for his cheesy shit. I'd hate to have to hear him brag about it.

I pull out my phone and open my Solitaire app. Sure, it feels good to have someone around that I can relate to, but there's no way in hell Josh and I will be friends. My douchebag radar is firing off at full speed. Hanging out with this guy would be like a giant contraceptive to any decent female.

I'M STANDING on the sidelines of a red carpet watching Willow situate Stella's dress until it's perfect. The black gown shows enough cleavage to make my dick stir but not so much that she might have a nip-slip if she makes the wrong move.

Willow explained my duties to me while Stella got ready for the show. My job is to stay by Stella's side yet remain unseen.

Stella runs her hand down her glossy jet-black hair, and the diamond bracelet around her wrist glistens. She struts the red carpet in her high heels like a pro, and it takes only a second for her to get into her perfect pose. The flash of cameras all going off at once hurts my eyes. They're afraid to miss a shot of her.

Paparazzi are squashed up like sardines behind a red rope that blocks them from her, and there are other security guards placed in every direction. Josh stops at my side at the same time I get a view of Eli.

Eli reminds me of a frat boy even though he's in his late twenties. Right now, he's sporting a cocky smile, his blond hair is gelled and combed to the side like a kid who stole his mom's beauty products, and he's wearing a black pinstriped suit that fits his skinny stature.

Josh slaps my back. "Let the madness begin, my friend."

I only nod in response.

I watch Eli pose for a few pictures and hold my breath when he moves into Stella's space. Stella's lips curve into a smile when he wraps his arm around her waist and drags her to his side. She tilts her hips toward him and rests her hand on his chest like a prom picture. The cameras go off like wildfire.

I cock my head to the side in confusion and scratch my cheek when Eli dips down and kisses her on the lips.

What am I missing here?

Stella and Eli barely exchanged three words on the flight. Eli sat next to Josh, and I tuned them out after they started arguing about what model was the most bangable on Instagram. Eli wasn't in her hotel suite when she got ready, and nobody mentioned him staying there tonight. Maybe they're in an open relationship type shit.

"Stella!" a woman screams when Eli grabs Stella's hand and walks her down the carpet. "How long have you two been dating?"

Neither of them answers her question.

"Eli!" another person blurts out. "Do you think your romance will continue when you finish promoting the movie?"

Stella and Eli make puppy eyes at each other before Eli leads her to the crowd of people waiting. "Our relationship will stay strong long after it ends," he responds before kissing Stella on the cheek. "I love her. She loves me, and that's all you need to know. Now, if you'll excuse us, we have a good ass movie to watch."

I force a smile when Stella and Eli reach me, and Willow rushes over to us with an annoyed look on her face.

"I hope it was worth it," she says to Stella, louder than I think she intended to.

"Don't start with me right now," Stella snaps.

"Whatever," Willow says, rolling her eyes. She looks at me while we file into the theater. "We're in the row behind the two lovebirds. I hope you have a thing for romance films."

I chuckle. "They're my favorite. Can't live without them."

"How'd I know you are a romantic at heart?"

"Definitely strikes me as the type," Stella comments, looking back at us and winking.

Stella sits next to Eli, and I take the seat behind her.

I'M NOT a romance film dude.

I fucking swear it.

The movie has my attention, and it's not because the storyline is kick-ass.

It's because of Stella.

I'm watching her every second, my gaze bouncing from the unreality of her on the movie screen to the reality of her in front of me. Eli's arm is settled on her shoulders, and I can't figure out why seeing him touch her *on- and off*-screen makes my blood boil.

I shake my head in an attempt to reason with myself.

There's no way I can be into this chick.

I'm only agitated because nothing is adding up.

I glance over at Willow next to me when her phone goes off again. It's been nonstop for the past ten minutes.

"You better answer that," I whisper. "It sounds important."

"Shit," she groans and roughly drags her phone from her pocket. "Everyone knows I'm here." She encloses her hand around the phone screen to block out the light and lets out a whimper. Her hand shakes as she types out a reply.

"Is everything okay?"

She keeps the screen covered but lowers her hand enough for me to read the text.

Mom: Brett got into a car accident. It's bad. You need to come home ASAP.

"Brett is my boyfriend," she says, close to tears. "This isn't good. I don't know what to do."

I give her a comforting look. "You go be with him."

"What about Stella?"

"I'll explain to her what happened and help out in any way I can in your place." I signal to the exit I scoped out when we walked in.

Willow squeezes my arm. "Thank you, Hudson. I'll do everything I can via phone and email until I figure out what's going on. Don't tell her why I left until the movie is over, okay? She'll freak out and try to come with me. That can't happen."

CHAPTER SEVEN

Stella

MY CHEST IS TIGHT. My jaw is tight. My muscles are tight.

"I can't believe you sat through the movie and didn't tell me," I yell at Hudson in the back hallway of the theater. He pulled me to the side minutes ago to tell me about Brett.

"I would've gone with her," I continue. "Call me a car. Hopefully, I can make it to the airport before her departure."

Willow has always been my rock. She was there for me during my breakup with Knox and when my so-called friends chose him over me. I wasn't good enough for them any longer. I hate that I can't be there with her now.

"Your reaction is why we didn't tell you," Hudson answers. "She didn't want you to get worked up like you are right now."

That's Willow—always putting my career before everything else.

"Of course, I'd get worked up! Something terrible happened to my best friend!"

His face softens.

"We need to figure this out."

"You make the call. If you want to fly to her, I'm game."

I stiffen when arms wrap around my waist from behind.

"You ready to head to the after-party?" Eli asks. "It's at this kick-ass exclusive club."

I peek back at Eli to see his face lit up in excitement.

Eli is a partier who goes through money and women like they're nothing. That's why they pressured me into playing his girlfriend. I'm looked at as the perfect role model. I'm the childhood star who didn't go wild and the perfect solution to the up-and-coming actor's bad-boy image.

I pull away from him and try to look disappointed. "Unfortunately, I have to bail. Willow's boyfriend got in a serious car accident, and I need to be with her."

"That won't be happening, Stella."

My heart races, and I groan at the sound of the high-strung voice that belongs to Tillie Armstrong, the pain in my ass with a stick up her ass who always seems to hit a nerve. She stops in front of me clad in a purple dress with her honey blond hair straightened to her shoulders.

"There was an agreement when you were given the movie part," Tillie reminds me. "Per your contract, you are required to attend all movie premieres with Eli *and* after-parties. In case you forgot, you signed the dotted line and must adhere to those obligations."

Tillie is the bitch … I mean *publicist* of the production company that funded our movie. Her favorite hobby is reminding me I'm contractually obligated to be their bitch. *Contractually obligated* makes up ninety percent of her vocabulary. I'm sure she says it in her sleep. She lurks, waiting to dispute my every move.

I'm contractually obligated to kiss Eli, to act like we're screwing, and declare my love for him. I wish I were contractually obligated to stick my stiletto up her ass.

"It's a family emergency," Hudson cuts in.

Tillie gives him an annoyed look. "I don't know who you are, nor do I care, but you're wrong. It's not a family emergency. It's someone else's family emergency. No relation. No excuses."

Hudson holds out his hand, his jaw clenching. "Then allow me to introduce myself. I'm Hudson, Stella's bodyguard. Now, you know who I am."

I bite into my lip and stare at him, loving how he's standing up to her.

"Pleasure," Tillie says, not bothering to shake his hand or introduce herself.

Hudson doesn't let her attitude stop him. He jerks his hand over to gesture to me. "You're going to make her stay here and do this shit when you can clearly see she's upset and wants to be there for her friend?"

"You must not understand contracts, Henry." Tillie looks over at me. "Show up to the party, or you'll be reaping the consequences."

"You must not have heard me. It's Hudson," he corrects.

Tillie snarls her lip. She's not used to people going to battle against her.

"Can't she miss one party?" Eli asks before Tillie decides to claw Hudson's eyes out. "I'll go with her to see Willow. It'll make me look like a supportive boyfriend."

Tillie shakes her head. "Neither one of you is going anywhere but that club. Period. This conversation is over." She gives us one last sharp look and leaves.

I fiddle with my bracelet. "Thanks for having my back and trying," I say to the guys, giving them a forced smile. I'm filled with devastation but trying to keep my cool. I'm an actress. I can do this.

Eli squeezes my shoulders in apology. "Sorry, babe. I'll do my best to get us out of the party as early as I can, if that helps?"

I nod. "Thank you."

"I need to find my manager and let him know what's going on," Eli says before disappearing down the hall.

"Who the fuck was that hag?" Hudson asks.

"That's the woman who holds my future in her hands and uses it as leverage anytime I don't fall in her line." I drop my arms at my sides. "She's the reason they gave me this role."

"Fuck her. That's bullshit." He stops to pull his phone from his pocket when it chimes. "It's Willow. She has fifteen minutes before her flight takes off. You want to give her a call?"

Tears fill my eyes, and I nod.

He hands me his phone, and I immediately hit Willow's name. She's sobbing when she answers. It hurts. I ask her over and over again if she wants me to come with her, but she refuses. She knows the hell Tillie will put me through if I bail. I make her promise to call or text when she lands and to keep me updated before hanging up.

"She good?" Hudson asks.

"As good as she can be," I answer. "Brett is in ICU, and her mom said it isn't looking good. She also said there are stories already floating around that he was drinking and driving and ran a stop sign."

"Fucking dumbass. How do they know that already?"

"A half-empty bottle of vodka was in the passenger seat. The hospital took a blood tox, but the results haven't come back yet."

"Shit. Poor Willow."

"That's not even the worst part."

His brows snap together.

"The car he hit was a mini-van with a family of four inside. They're not sure if one of the children will survive."

"Fuck. That has to be a lot for her to take in."

Brett drinking and driving doesn't surprise me. He's not a good guy, but Willow refuses to leave him. They've been on and off since high school, and she can't walk away because of their history, even though it's not a healthy relationship.

Something hits me when I look back at Hudson.

We're going to be alone in the hotel tonight.

Uh-oh.

Being in a hotel is different than my home, where thousands of square feet separate us. I didn't plan on drinking at tonight's after-party, but a stiff drink is sounding pretty damn good right now.

CHAPTER EIGHT

Hudson

"I'LL SUCK your cock if you let me through."

I stare at the half-naked girl who can't be any older than eighteen standing in front of me. "What did you just say?"

Another woman, a twin I'm assuming, comes to her side, and they both look up at me with innocent brown eyes.

Fuck.

I want to take them home to their parents.

How did they even get in here?

It's been one long ass day, and it keeps getting stranger by the second.

The after-party is in a club filled with dancers and women serving overpriced drinks. To be honest, it's giving me a damn headache.

When did I turn into an old man?

I enjoy having a good time, watching live bands, and drinking beers with my friends, but this shit is a madhouse. People are bumping into each other, screaming in faces, and girls are fighting their way into the VIP section like Stella and Eli are a fucking king and queen.

They remind me of roaches. I block one chick from

sneaking in, and there's another one sliding into my left. No way are any of these groupie vultures going near my cock.

STD-free is the way I want to be.

Josh steps to my side with a disturbing smile on his face. "If he's not game, I am."

Of course, he is.

Dude will fuck anything if it means he doesn't go to bed alone with his sausage link in his hand. He's dumb to think these women actually want him. They look at him as a stepping stool to a better opportunity … Eli.

"How about you two make out and we'll consider if you're worthy of our time," he tells them.

My skin crawls at his creepiness.

I gesture to them. "Dude, they're fucking twins who look sixteen. Incest and pedophilia your thing?" *Sick fuck.*

He chuckles. "They're not *my* sisters, and obviously if they're here, they're old enough." He leans back on his heels, crosses his arms, and licks his lips. "I've always wanted to fuck twins. There's something so hot about it."

"Hot?" I repeat. "I think you meant to say fucking gross."

"Lighten up. We're all here to have a little fun."

The girls are staring at us with expectation and waiting for their golden ticket.

"We're eighteen," one says, grinning wildly. "Legal as can be."

I scowl at how pathetic they sound and look over at Josh. "Have fun with your cock-sucking sisters. I'll be over here doing my job and relishing in the fact I won't have to visit the clinic tomorrow."

He shrugs. "More pussy for me then."

I shudder. "Enjoy it while it lasts because I have a feeling your dick will be fall off in the next few years."

I walk away and lean back against a wall. I'm ready to blow this joint and hit the sheets. I glance over at Stella and Eli to find them whispering sweet nothings into each other's ears.

Why are these other women trying to get to Eli?

Stella has his full attention. It's obvious they'll be leaving together. Hopefully, they'll have their fun in his suite.

Their relationship confuses me. Stella didn't seem interested in him all day. She doesn't even look happy now as she chugs down drinks and stares into space. She rolls her eyes when Eli starts raining kisses down her neck but still tilts her head to the side to give him better access.

There's no enjoyment on her face.

He's not getting her all hot and bothered.

It can't be what it seems.

I LET OUT a breath of relief when Stella informs me that she's ready to leave.

My head is dying for some silence, and I swear if another chick offers me sex, I'm going to throw her out of the club.

I never thought I'd be bitching about being offered pussy. Yet, here I am. The worst part is that I have to wake up and do it all over again tomorrow.

Thankfully, the suite we're staying in is in the same building as the club. I have to help Stella walk back, and she wobbles in my hold. The alcohol hitting her doesn't surprise me. She spent her night competing against herself over how many drinks she could suck down.

I shut the door behind us and walk through the foyer of the decked-out suite. Stella lives a life of luxury. The suite is spacious and the décor expensive. I have my own bedroom and private bathroom, even though I'd prefer more privacy. I shared a bedroom and bathroom with dozens of other men for months. Some space would be nice.

I asked Stella several times if she wanted me to take her to Eli's room, but she only shook her head and muttered something along the lines of, "Over my dead body."

"Are you sure you don't want to stay with your boyfriend?" I ask again.

She collapses on the couch and starts fumbling with the strap of her sparkly heel, stumbling in the process. I should help her, but that's not my job. I'm here to make sure she's not kidnapped or murdered, not to help her do shit like that. She throws the heel down when she's successful, and it takes her a few seconds to gain control of herself to start working on the other.

"My boyfriend?" she says when she manages to get it off.

I recline against the wall and watch her. "The dude you were all over at the theater? The one you were tonsil scrubbing with at the club?"

How drunk is this broad?

"Eli?" Her face turns horrified when I nod. "Gross. He isn't my boyfriend."

"Fine, your fuck buddy."

"We sure as hell aren't *fucking*. We're fake dating."

The fuck? Who does that?

I rub the back of my neck, replaying her response like I misheard it. "Why would you fake date someone?"

It's the most absurd shit I've heard all day. Hell, maybe all year. And I've had one eventful year.

She leans back and waves her hand through the air. "It's complicated."

Complicated yet captivating.

I shove my hands into the pockets of my jeans and prepare myself for story time. This is something I can't wait to hear. "Sounds like it. I can listen to complicated."

"You're going to find out eventually," she mutters, looking anxious. "We're pretending to date to promote our movie. You know, drive up publicity and hype. His camp wants his reputation cleaned up because he's been somewhat of a loose cannon and man slut. They look at me as the perfect child star all grown up, so it was either I agree and get the role, or they find someone else to go along with it. I decided to advance my career."

I can't hold in my laugh, and her brows furrow at me.

"You're a rent-a-girlfriend?"

People actually do that shit?

It dawns on me now that was what that Tillie chick was referring to. She's in a contract to date Eli.

She grimaces at my comparison. "Don't say it like that."

"Why? It sounds better than me saying you're pimping yourself out for the success of your movie."

"Thanks, I appreciate you calling me a hooker."

"I didn't call you anything, Hollywood."

"You insinuated it."

"I guess so, but it's not exactly my business." I point at the door. "You sure you don't want me to leave? You can call Eli over, tip off paparazzi, and it'll look like you two are in here making sweet love when in actuality you'll be sexting other people from opposite ends of the couch." I grin. "Perfect relationship, if you ask me. Very romantic."

My crudeness surprises her. It surprises me, too.

She frowns. "Has anyone ever told you you're an asshole?"

I place my hand over my heart and lower my voice. "My feelings … stop."

I *am* acting like an asshole, but I'm mad at myself. I was changing my mind about Stella being a selfish brat after our talk in the kitchen and seeing her reaction to Willow's situation, but I was wrong.

She snatches her clutch and starts rummaging through it like a madwoman until she finds her phone. "I'm texting Willow and telling her to find a replacement for you immediately."

"Good riddance. My prayers have been answered. The sooner, the better."

"Why don't you quit then? Why even take the job if I repulse you so much?"

"My brother begged me to, and the last thing he needs at

the moment is to be stressed about you being unprotected," I pause and tilt my head toward the phone in her hand. "And it's probably a bad idea to text Willow right now."

Some of her anger dissipates as her shoulders slump. "Good point. I'd be freaking out if something like that happened to my boyfriend."

"Your real boyfriend or a fake one? Can you be more specific so I can keep up?"

She flips me off. "You're an ass, and I'm speaking in generality. No boyfriend here. I'm officially on a break from dating."

"Unless you're getting a paycheck for it?"

"Go screw yourself. I'm fake dating for the sake of my career, and it's not the first time it's been done. I'm sure it won't be the last either."

"You might be right, but it's the first time I've known someone to. Where I come from, we don't date for paychecks. We tend to call those people hookers … street walkers …"

"I don't live *where you come from*, so how about that? *Where I come from*, we focus on our careers and people don't insult their bosses." She gets up from the couch to stomp to her bedroom and turns around to give me one last scowl before going in. "Keep your mouth shut about Eli. You can't tell your friends, girlfriend, anyone."

"You don't have to worry about that." I use my hand to form a zipping gesture across my mouth. "These lips are sealed."

CHAPTER NINE

Stella

I SLAM the door and dramatically collapse on my bed, pouting like a three-year-old whose blankie is in the dryer.

I'm drunk and overreacting but hearing the truth from Hudson hurt. He only confirmed what I've been afraid of from the start of signing off on this deal. I'm pimping myself out for the sake of my career and money.

I've tried telling myself it's not bad because I'm not screwing Eli.

Isn't it only hooking if you're fucking and sucking someone?

So, I'm in the clear, right?

Now, I need to convince my Hudson-altered conscience that.

Men are a pain in the ass.

Which is exactly why I've sworn them off.

They might come with a good penis, but there's always a side dish of problems.

A situation like this would usually warrant a call to Willow where I'd rant about how big of an asshole Hudson is. She'd tell me to kick him in the nuts or let it go depending on her mood.

I can't do that tonight. She's going through too much, and it would be selfish of me to bother her with something this petty.

Unlocking my phone, I scroll down to Dallas's name. Maybe he can talk some manners into his jerk of a brother.

For a moment, I thought Hudson and I were moving in the right direction, maybe even starting to like each other. We had the whole late-night kitchen conversation, we flirted, and he stuck up for me with Tillie.

Apparently, I was wrong.

My finger hovers over Dallas's name, but I stop myself.

It'd be selfish calling him.

Well, damn.

Who can I call and complain to?

Who can I ask for advice?

I hit my sister, Antonia's, name. It rings several times before going to voicemail. She's probably busy. She signed a modeling contract six months ago and has been touring the globe for fashion shows.

I slap my forehead and know I've hit rock bottom when I call my mother.

Don't get me wrong. I love her.

The problem is I'm not sure if she loves me or only sees me as her meal ticket. We talked regularly, and she was my biggest fan until Knox and I broke up. She begged me to get back with him for the sake of my career and was furious when I refused.

My call goes straight to voicemail.

No *shocker.*

I contemplate calling an old friend but decide against it. I'm so out of touch with that circle. Most of them took Knox's side in the breakup. He's richer and has more connections than I do.

All invites and calls stopped coming my way after he told our friends he didn't want me around because he had a new girlfriend. Hollywood friends see you as disposable.

I toss my phone down and sigh. This should to be the peak of my career, but I feel so alone.

Tears fall down my cheek, and desperation leads me to grab my phone and hit the last name I should.

Me: YOU ARE AN ASSHOLE AND NEED TO WORK ON YOUR PEOPLE SKILLS AND MANNERS!

There.

I said what I needed to.

I put my phone down and pick up a magazine sitting on the nightstand. My phone beeps before I make it past the first article. I drop the magazine and take a deep breath before looking at the screen.

Hudson: Are you text-sulting me from the next room? Put on your big girl panties and stomp your spoiled ass out here if you want to scream at me. All caps aren't necessary. They don't do your entitled temper justice.

Ugh, the nerve of this jackass.

Text-sulting? Who even says that?

I swing my legs over the edge of the bed, jump off, and stomp my unspoiled ass back into the living room. Hudson is situated comfortably on the couch with not a care in the world.

Did our argument not even faze him?

"Temper?" I scream. "You want to see a temper?"

His arms are crossed, and a smile dances over his lips. "Go ahead, Hollywood. Temper away. Stomp your feet. Do whatever you feel is necessary to prove you're different than what the headlines say."

Why does he have a good comeback for everything?

I want to shock him, make him at a loss for words, and show him I'm a force to be reckoned with.

I point at him. "You need to start being nice, or I'll tell Dallas to inform your girlfriend how big of a dick you're being."

Yes, I suck at comebacks. I sound like a tattletale on the playground.

Hudson laughs while looking more entertained. "Let me know how that goes, will you? I have a feeling she'll be too busy fucking my best friend than worry about who I'm supposedly insulting."

My mouth slams shut.

His grin grows. "Not the response you were expecting?"

I was right about him no longer being in a relationship.

Embarrassment sweeps up my cheeks. "I thought you were engaged?"

Should this new information excite me?

It does.

"I was. Not anymore. Cameron decided she liked to screw my best friend, and I'm not one to share pussy. When I make someone mine, they're mine. Sharing is not always caring."

His answer sends shivers down my spine. My heart races over the way he talks about ownership.

"That sucks. I'm sorry," is the only response I can muster out after throwing a failed relationship in his face.

He shrugs. "Shit happens and you move on."

I walk farther into the room and sit down in a chair, wanting him to continue. *Give me more! Unleash your secrets!*

"How long were you two engaged?"

"We dated twelve years. Engaged three."

"Wow. That's a long time."

My final breakup with Knox crushed me. We dated on and off for almost a decade. I can't imagine how I'd feel if I found out he was sleeping with my best friend.

Friendship code 101: Don't fuck each other's exes.

Male or female.

Not even if the dude is young *Fight Club* era Brad Pitt.

They're off-limits.

If you do, you were never a true friend to begin with.

There are millions of cocks and vaginas in the world. It's not hard to find one that hasn't been with your best friend.

I take a deep breath and shove my hand out his way. "Can we call a truce?"

He looks at me skeptically. "You mean you're done calling me an asshole?"

"As long as you quit referring to me as a hooker."

"Fine, truce." He shakes my hand, and I'm disappointed at the loss of his touch when he releases me. "All hooker comments will be kept to myself."

"And stop *thinking* of me as a hooker, too. I'm not sleeping with Eli."

He taps his chin. "Do you know the definition of hooker?"

"Can't say it's something I've looked up before." I raise a brow. "Do you?"

I wait for him to spit out some Webster's Dictionary definition that confirms you don't have to sleep with someone to be defined as a hooker.

He laughs. It's deep and manly. "I'm only fucking with you, Hollywood. Consider all hooker-talk done. I promise."

I tip my head down. "Thank you."

"My hooker-ending talking pleasure."

I give him a hard look.

He laughs again while holding up his hands. "Last one, I swear."

I stand but stagger for a moment to gain my balance. "I need another drink."

The slight-buzz I have from the after-party is still drumming through me. That must be why I'm so emotional. Alcohol is like a therapist. It puts you in your feelings until eventually, you blurt out everything that's bothering you.

"You sure that's a good idea?" He sits up and scoots to the end of the couch like he knows he'll have to save me from busting my ass.

"Positive." I snag a pint of vodka when I make it to the minibar and mix it with a Coke before turning around and looking at him. I hold out my tongue and cough after swallowing down the first drink. *This stuff is not for the weak.* I hold up my drink. "What's your cocktail of choice?"

Alcohol drops my inhibitions. Maybe it will do the same for him.

He shakes his head. "I don't drink on the job."

"Then prepare to never drink while working for me since you'll pretty much always be on the job." I hold the bottle in front of me. "What if I said you're off the clock?"

His brows squeeze together. "I'm still good. It's three in the morning, and I'm exhausted."

"You're going to make me drink alone?"

My heart races when he stands up and advances my way. "Tell you what, Princess Peer Pressure, I'll have one beer if that makes you feel better. That's it."

It's no surprise he's a beer drinker.

I catch my breath when he walks around me to open the fridge and take him in while he's not looking at me. His hair smells like fake ocean breeze shampoo, and oddly, I find that attractive. I've been around so many men who pour on expensive cologne and use shampoo products so strong they give you a headache. It's nice for a man to smell like a man.

I jump and look at him in embarrassment when he pops off the cap of the bottle. He smirks, fully aware I'd been checking him out, and takes long strides to the couch like he's trying to get as far away from me as possible.

"What do we do now?" he asks, sitting down. "Drink and stare at each other?"

I collapse into the chair again. "I didn't think that far ahead. I can't sleep and need something to take my mind off my life."

"Your life that bad, huh?" His hand wraps around the neck of the bottle while gently tipping it against his lips.

"Don't patronize me. I'm not saying I'm impoverished."

"What will help take your mind off your *very* serious problems?"

I hold up my drink. "More alcohol. Mindless chatter." I angle my body toward him. "An *orgasm.*" I shrug. "Maybe two."

I don't know who's more shocked at my response—him or me. I try to appear calm, but my heart is beating like crazy.

He points at me with his beer. "I'll take mindless chatter for four hundred."

That sucks. I was hoping for option three.

I throw my arms out. "Then let's chat away."

"Why don't we get to know each other since we'll be spending a lot of time together? It'd be nice to know I'm not hanging out with a serial killer."

I perk up in my seat and keep sipping on my drink. "How exactly do you suggest we get to know each other?"

He smirks. "Not like that, you little perv."

I put my hand over my heart, feigning offense. "Me? A perv?"

He chuckles. "Alcohol makes you more open. I like it."

"Hopefully, it's the same with you. You're like a sealed up, boring box."

"I'm not an emotional guy who expresses his feelings. Maybe that's why Cameron decided to cheat on me. She wanted some sappy dude who sang love ballads and shit. I'm not that guy."

I snort. "A man who sings love ballads doesn't mean they're sappy or even a good boyfriend. My ex is a master in songwriting and belting out love songs, and it didn't make our relationship stronger. It only made the fan girls want to suck his cock more and gave me insecurities. They don't tell you that love songs aren't made for love. They're made for money."

"The child star has quite the potty mouth."

"Profanity is my dominant language when I'm drunk. Don't judge me."

"No judging here. I like a girl who talks dirty."

My eyes widen, and he shakes his head when he realizes what he said.

Looks like we're both saying the wrong things to each other.

"Shit, I didn't mean it like that. I've never had a job like this, but I'm working on keeping it as professional as I can."

"Professionalism is dull." Yep, I'm officially getting drunker and braver with every sip.

"Consider our relationship dull then."

"You suck," I slur. The alcohol is making me dizzy, and I move back and forth in my chair.

He stands. "I think it's time for you to go to bed, drunkie."

"Oh come, on," I whine. "Your job is not to be a party pooper."

"My job is to take care of you."

"Oh, I know *plenty* of ways you can take care of me." I can't help but stare at his crotch when he stops in front of me. I lick my lips. "Plenty of fun ways."

I'm single. He's single.

The perfect situation for my abandoned vagina.

Maybe Willow was right.

I know I said all men are off-limits, but the appeal of Hudson getting me off tonight is changing my mind. My heart goes crazy when he helps me to my feet to stand on my own.

Okay, stumble on my own.

He grunts when I fall against his hard chest and circles his arm around my waist to stop me from busting my ass. For some idiotic reason, I take it as an invite to kiss him. I stand on my tiptoes and smack my lips into his briefly before he snags my wrists and nudges me away.

Big mistake.

Big freaking mistake.

He rests his hands on my shoulders, making sure I'm balanced but keeping distance between us, and stares at me with what looks like pity. I curl my arms around my stomach and dip my chin down to the floor.

He clears his throat before speaking. "It's time to call it a night." He forces a laugh in an attempt to make me feel less humiliated, but it doesn't work.

I run my hands down my dress. My embarrassment is erasing my intoxication.

"Can we act like this never happened?" I whisper, my voice cracking. I'm ready to go to my room and suffocate myself out of shame.

"We can definitely do that." Just like the first time we met, he looks like he'd rather be anywhere but here.

I want to stop the next words from flying from my mouth, but I can't. "I know it'd be so embarrassing for you to hook up with someone like me."

His jaw ticks, and his face shifts from apologetic to agitation. "The fuck you mean someone like you?"

"Someone like me," I repeat. "Don't think I don't see the way you look at me. You don't see *me.*" I tap my hand against my chest while fighting back fresh tears. "You only see the headlines, the stories, what you think you know and feel as if it's beneath you to be attracted to someone so shallow."

His voice drops. "There's no way you can think I feel like I'm too good for you. I didn't stop you because of that. We can't cross that line. You're drunk. I work for you. I'm sorry if I gave you the wrong idea."

"It's fine. I'm sorry, and you're right." I finally gain the courage to look at him. "Can I ask you a question?"

He shoots me a guarded smile. "Go for it."

"Do you think what I'm doing is wrong?"

I know what his response will be. He expressed his disgust for it earlier, but *maybe* I changed his mind … even if just a little.

"Please be honest with me."

"I think fake dating someone sounds absurd, but we live in two different worlds. I know nothing about the Hollywood life. If you feel like that's what you have to do for your career, that's all that matters. I won't lie and say it doesn't sound desperate, but again, it's your life. That's me being honest with you. Now come on, let's get you to bed."

I nod, and he takes my hand to lead me down the hallway. I stay quiet while he lifts back the blankets on my bed and waits for me to get in before turning off the light and leaving.

I don't know what storm is suddenly brewing inside me, but I have a feeling Hudson is the force behind it.

CHAPTER TEN

Hudson

LEANING BACK against the door to my bedroom, I go over what just happened with Stella.

I walk to the side of the bed and hold my hands out in front of me, studying them and remembering how soft her skin felt against my calloused palms. It almost feels wrong for something so rough to touch something so delicate.

I close my eyes and remember her reaction to me touching her. I haven't been laid in so long. *Two hundred and seventy days to be exact, but hey, who's counting?* It killed me to walk away from something so damn tempting.

Most guys would call me a fucking idiot.

Hell, I'm calling myself a fucking idiot.

I drag my shirt over my head, throw it across the room, and peek down at the tent in my pants. I wanted nothing more than to push her onto the couch and give us what we both ached for. The attraction is there—there's no denying that—but I can't cross that line. I have a job to do, and I won't be able to concentrate on protecting her if all I can think about is how sweet her pussy tastes.

No drinking with Stella.

No hanging out with a drunk Stella.

No personal stories and opening up to each other.

We want different things.

There's no way I can sleep with her and then watch Eli touch her after. I can't sit to the side while they act like they're screwing if I'm screwing her. What confuses me the most is why I'm crushing on a liar who's fake dating someone to further her career.

I fucking hate liars.

I grab my laptop and mute the sound. Even though I want to listen, she can't know what I'm doing. Wearing headphones isn't an option either. *What if someone breaks in?* If something happens to her, it wouldn't be cool for people to find out I was jerking my dick to porn instead of doing my job.

I pull my cock from my shorts and slowly stroke myself.

Fuck. This feels so good.

Thank God for Porn Hub.

CHAPTER ELEVEN

Stella

REGRET POUNDS through my skull when I wake up.

Humiliation is riding at its side, pointing and laughing at me.

I'm embarrassed I offered myself up to Hudson, and he rejected me.

Insanity convinced me that us sharing a drink meant he wanted to screw me.

It's been so long since I've put myself out there like that to someone. It'll never happen again after his rejection. Not only is it a smack to my ego but it's also a slap to my senses for thinking it's okay to get involved with my bodyguard.

I want to be angry with him but can't.

Hudson did the right thing.

At least one of our brains was working last night.

I notice mascara streaks on my pillow. I cried last night and forgot to take off my makeup. *Here come the wrinkles to go along with my mortification.*

I enter the bathroom, wipe the mascara from my face, and climb in the shower. The steam helps to cleanse my pores of the extra alcohol and minimize my hangover. I run my fingers through the thick strands of my wet hair when I get out, wrap them in a tight bun, and start my walk of shame into the kitchen. Hudson is sitting at the table drinking coffee with a laptop open in front of him.

I don't look in his direction while heading straight to the coffee maker and jump when he speaks.

"Morning. How are you feeling?"

"Like I was living it up riding roller coasters all night," I mutter.

Maybe I can act like I don't remember last night. I gear up for the perfect *I did what?* look.

I'm an actress. I got this.

I pull out a mug from the cabinet with the hotel's logo, and my hands are trembling when I pour coffee inside it. I look around the room while taking small sips, not sure what to do.

He gets straight to the point. "About last night."

"What about last night?" I ask.

"I can tell by your face that you know exactly what I'm talking about."

I frown. "God, even bringing it up makes my head hurt. Can we not do this right now … or say, maybe never?"

"Not talking about it will only make it more awkward."

"Fine, but you're going first."

He tips his finger toward the seat across from him. "Sit down."

"Seriously? You're going to make this all weird and personal?"

"You standing there looking uncomfortable as fuck is making it weird."

"Who decided you were the boss man all of a sudden?" I complain but do as told.

He sits back in his chair and clears his throat. "First things first. I hope you don't feel like I rejected you last night."

I scoff. "Too late for that."

"You're beautiful, and you have to know I'm attracted to you."

I raise a brow. *News to me.*

If this is his attempt to keep our relationship professional, it's not working. His admission makes me only want him more.

"You were drunk, and we're both lonely. I should've never allowed it to go that far."

"Speak for yourself. I'm not lonely."

His look causes me to slam my mouth shut.

He can read me like a damn script.

I perk up in my chair and settle my hands on the table. "I don't like where this conversation is going. It was a drunken mishap. Let's forget about it and move on."

"Fine with me. I only wanted to clear the air."

I swipe my hands together. "Consider it cleared." I pick up my phone. "Do you want anything from room service?" I forgot to order my breakfast last night. Willow usually does that for me, but I sent her a text telling her I'd have everything taken care of.

"Whatever you order is fine with me."

I order our food and start to answer emails and texts while he stays occupied with his computer. I open a message from Willow giving me an update on Brett's condition. His recovery isn't promising, and she's not sure how long she'll be gone.

My stomach drops at the resignation letter attached to the email. I message her back, insisting she take as much time off as she needs and her job will be waiting for her when she's ready to come back. Hudson allows room service in, and the sweet aroma of pastries and pancakes fills the room and causes my stomach to growl.

Hudson takes a bite of pancakes and groans. "Damn, this shit is good. I've missed food like this."

I nod even though I haven't touched my food. A question is eating at me. A question that's none of my business.

"How long has it been since you've been with a woman?" I ask.

Hudson nearly chokes on his food but doesn't hesitate to answer. "A little over nine months."

"You didn't screw someone the second you got home?"

"I was more interested in seeing my family than getting my dick wet. Not to mention, had I screwed someone, that news would've been all over our small town, given my situation with Cameron."

"I thought my drought was sad."

"Not a drought, Hollywood. It's lack of opportunity."

Lack of opportunity? There was opportunity with me last night.

"What are you going on?"

"Two months," I admit.

He grins and shakes his head. "Amateur."

Lord, give me courage for what I'm about to say and help a girl out if you can.

"Can I ask you something, and you promise to take me seriously?"

He cocks his head to the side. "Sure."

"I know only thirty minutes ago, you said you want to keep our relationship professional …"

"I did."

"But what will throwing a little sex hurt?" I sound like a horny teenage boy who's the only one in gym class who hasn't had his cock sucked.

His voice deepens. "Bad idea."

"Why not have some fun? Haven't you ever had a one-night stand?"

His gaze closes in on me. "I've only been with one woman."

I nearly drop my coffee. Hudson continues to shock me.

What do they feed these guys in Iowa?

"You're lying."

He shakes his head. "I started dating Cameron in middle school and never touched anyone but her. Your proposition sounds nice, but I'm a selfish guy. I've never had to separate commitment and sex, and I'm not sure if I'd be okay touching you one night and then watching you suck face with Eli the next day."

"What if you can separate it? Why not try?"

"Dump the phony boyfriend, and maybe I'll broaden my horizons."

With that, he stands up, grabs his mug, and leaves the room.

"THIS SHIT FUCKING BLOWS," Eli says, plopping down in the seat next to me after boarding the plane. We're headed to London for the next premiere.

"What blows?" I ask.

I don't know Eli that well, which is weird, considering I've made out with him on-screen, and there are rumors we're screwing off-screen. He reminds me of my ex—nice guy but also a playboy eager to cross every Victoria's Secret model off his screw list.

Since agreeing to be his fake girlfriend, my life has been nothing but chaos. We've received backlash from not only fans but also mutual friends. Knox and Eli had been friends, and they saw that as a broken vow of bros before hoes. It's ridiculous, considering Knox gives two shits about who I'm sleeping with.

"Fake dating," Eli answers. "It's putting a damper on my sex life."

I roll my eyes. "Gee, thanks. I'm having the time of my life."

He chuckles. "It's not you. It's me."

I place my hand over my heart. "Tragic. I'm so heartbroken. Now, go tell Tillie about our breakup. I'm as ready to end this deal as you."

He smirks. "Or we can try a different route?"

"We kill Tillie?"

"I'm too pretty for prison, sweetheart." He shoots me a confident grin. "I was thinking more along the lines of us *actually* dating."

I smack him upside the head. "Not happening. Everyone knows your dating record is worse than Charlie Sheen's."

"Whoa, a little overboard there. I don't mean us dating-dating."

"That's what it sounds like."

"Consider it more as colleagues with benefits."

I cringe. "You've lost your damn mind."

"Have I? Think about it. Neither of us is getting laid. Why not take advantage of the crappy situation we're in? I've had blue balls for months."

I don't believe he's been abstaining from sex. "Not happening." I've already had one Hollywood bad boy break my heart—putting myself at risk again would be stupid.

"Why not? Everyone already thinks we're screwing, so we might as well make the best of it."

"How about this. You are more than welcome to have fun with other people *behind closed doors.* Don't make me look like an idiot allowing her boyfriend to cheat. As long as it's on the down-low, I don't care what or who you do."

"Risk a picture or story being leaked? I won't ruin my career for a one-night fling."

I nod in agreement. "I won't tell if you don't."

He raises a brow. "Is that what you're doing? Sneaking around behind closed doors?"

"Uh, no."

He snorts. "Yeah, right."

"What are you trying to say?"

"I'm saying if I was your bodyguard, you'd be more than happy to accept my offer of sex."

Am I that obvious?

I put on my best innocent face. "What?"

He throws his head back and laughs. "Don't try to bullshit me. You've been giving him bedroom eyes all morning. Deny it all you want, but something's going on between you two."

"You're wrong."

"If you haven't fucked yet, it'll happen. All I'm asking is you make sure no cameras or witnesses are around. I won't be humiliated either." He scowls. "I've kept my dick in my pants and held up my end of the deal. Do the same."

He gets up to leave, but I stop him before he moves into the aisle.

"I can't," I say.

He looks down at me in confusion.

"I can't keep my dick in my pants, considering I don't have one."

"Fucking attitude," he grumbles. "I'll clarify, keep dicks out of you."

I squint my eyes. "Only dicks?"

"Jesus Christ, what else do you put inside yourself?"

I shrug.

Messing with him is fun.

"Maybe you're not the prude I thought you were."

"The hell?"

He hunches when I shove my elbow into his stomach.

"You think I'm a prude in the bedroom?"

"Obviously. You aren't interested in fucking me."

I grimace. "Check your ego, amigo. Me not wanting to screw you doesn't make me a prude."

"I'm beginning to see that, violent one." He pats my head. "My offer still stands. Let me know if you change your mind."

I let out a long sigh.

Hudson made it clear he'll only touch me if I ditch Eli.

Is a fling with him worth my career?

CHAPTER TWELVE

Hudson

"HEY! YOU! BODYGUARD GUY!"

I turn to find the hag who'd given Stella shit last night marching toward me. Stella and Eli boarded the jet a few minutes ago while I stayed in the car and took a call from Dallas.

I contemplate answering her but finally do. "Yeah?"

Her hands rest on her hips as she narrows her eyes at me, and she taps her heel against the ground. She appears as if she's readying to lecture a child.

That child being me.

Not fucking happening.

"Let me give you some words of advice," she snarls. "You seem to be confused about how this industry works and the respect you need to give to keep your job."

I could give two shits about keeping this job.

I flash her a cold smile. "I'm not trying to make a mark in this industry, and sure as fuck don't need any advice from you. Appreciate your concern, though."

"How about this. Let me give you some tips on how to stay on my good side."

I smirk. "I don't want to be on your good side. I quite enjoy being on the opposite."

Her face pinches. She's used to barking demands and having people bow down to her. No doubt she'll try to convince Stella to fire my ass. "You should be."

I move in, not close enough to be intimidating but enough to convince her I'm not one to fuck with. "Being on your good side is at the bottom of my give a shit list."

Her eyes widen.

"And while we're sharing wisdom, I have a tip for you."

She clears her throat. "What's that?"

"Get laid and stop making everyone's lives miserable." I gesture to the plane. "You denied Stella to visit her best friend whose boyfriend is on life support. Have some compassion, grow a heart, be a good fucking human being."

She looks me up and down with disgust clear on her face. "Sorry, but I don't take advice from nobodies."

"News flash, you're also a nobody. You bully people and make sure contracts are fulfilled, but you're not the star." I grin. "Welcome to the club. Now, I believe we have a flight to catch."

I leave without another word and board the plane. Josh and Eli are deep in conversation, and I take the seat next to Stella, which results in her peering at me in surprise.

I stretch my legs out in front of me. "How many of these things do we have to go to?"

There are only so many premieres you can have before the movie is old news, right?

"Only one more to go," she answers, moving her neck from side to side like it's sore. "It's a short promo tour. My guess is they weren't sure how long Eli and I could fake being a couple."

I lower my voice and tilt my head toward Eli. "What's the plan with lover boy? How long do you have to participate in this dating scheme?"

The conversation I had with her this morning haunts me. I

hate feeling this pull toward her *and* can't stop thinking about her.

She rolls her eyes. "I thought we were done talking about it?"

I hold up my hands. "I'm not trying to be a dick, I swear."

"That's a first."

"It's a valid question for someone who's involved."

"We have to attend all interviews and award shows together. There's a set date in the contract. I think we have eight months left."

"What if you decide you want out?"

"It will be a breach of contract, and they can sue me for more money than I made off the movie. Tillie will do everything in her power to destroy my career and reputation."

"Sounds like you signed a deal with the devil."

She shrugs. "It won't be that bad when we get back in LA. Eli is working on a movie being shot in a different state, so we won't have to fake it as much. My show is over, so I'll be auditioning for new roles. My life will be boring."

I nudge my foot against hers. "Hey, I like to think I'm a good time."

"Wrong. I *tried* to get you to be a good time, but you declined."

I bump my knee against hers next. "Fucking isn't the only way to have fun."

"Prove it then," she mutters.

Her challenging me only heightens my attraction, and I'm never one to back down from a challenge.

CHAPTER THIRTEEN

Stella

I WAS NEVER one of those kids who sat in front of the TV and dreamed of being on it one day. When teachers asked me what I wanted to be when I got older, it was never famous. Show business was more of my mother's dream that she never achieved, so she decided to live vicariously through me.

I hated doing commercials for toys and fast food restaurants. She once forced me to be in an ad for toilet paper. Instead, I wanted to be on the playground or at a sleepover with my friends, not attend every casting call in LA looking for a girl my age. The small roles changed when I turned fifteen and landed my first major gig on the pilot of a new show.

I loved my character, my castmates, and the production crew on the show. My mom didn't have to drag me out of bed and force me to go to work every day. It became my passion and what made me realize that maybe it was what I wanted to do with my life.

Unfortunately, we wrapped up our last season of the show a few months ago. Only so much time can pass before the kids get too old to live with their parents and storylines run out. The series ended with me finding the man of my dreams who also happened to be the head of the witching department at a prestigious school.

Too bad my life is the complete opposite.

Maybe that's why I liked it so much.

The cancellation of the show has me looking for the next role to fall in love with. I thought Sadie, the role I played in the movie with Eli, was it when I read the script. I was wrong. I see that now as I watch the movie for the sixth time that my heart wasn't in it.

We're at another screening, and I'm sure a migraine will hit me from smelling Eli's expensive cologne all night. I subtly look back at Hudson in the row behind us and wish I could replace Eli with him. I also wish I didn't want that.

Under no circumstances can I fall for my bodyguard.

That's so cliché.

So Heidi Klum after she divorced Seal.

I don't know of one celebrity–bodyguard romance that's worked out.

Why did Hudson have to slide into that open position?

He's loyal. Up-front. Real. Rare qualities in men as attractive as he is. Or maybe that's only in Hollywood. I should broaden my horizons.

Tillie will kill me. Eli will kill me. Dallas will probably kill me when things don't work out between his brother and me. I also don't see Hudson taking this job long term or staying in California. I can't give up my career and move to Cornfield Timbuktu.

I pinch myself, hoping it'll make me think more clearly. I'm daydreaming about moving to Hudson's hometown even though he's made it clear he wants nothing to do with me.

Willow is right. Lack of dick can make you delusional. When I get home, I'm dragging out my vibrator.

That will compensate enough, right?

It won't be as fun as a real cock and a hard body above me, nor can it eat me out, but hey, a girl has to get off some way.

Unless.

I can be persuasive.

My mind is toggling back and forth like two open internet tabs.

I want Hudson.

That's for sure.

But I *shouldn't* want him.

I *can't* want him.

I look up at the sound of applause, realizing I've zoned out for the entire movie.

"ARE we flying back to LA in the morning?" Hudson asks when we make it back to the suite from the after-party.

It's late, and I can't wait to take off my makeup and throw my ass into bed. You'd think someone my age would be excited to party all night, but I'm over it, especially now that I have to act like I'm obsessed with Eli the entire time.

Talk about a total buzzkill.

The buzzkill could've also been Hudson giving us a death stare the entire time we were playing boyfriend and girlfriend.

"We are," I answer. "Then we're taking a connecting flight to see Willow." Willow lives a few hours from LA.

"Any updates on her situation?"

"Brett is still on the ventilator. Other than that, nothing."

He nods.

We're standing in the living room only a few feet away from each other and having an awkward stare off. I tense at the sound of his throat clearing.

"We need to get to bed. We have a long day ahead of us tomorrow," he states.

I fiddle with my hands in front of me, still staring. In hopes I wouldn't make a fool of myself again, I chose to stay sober and only drink water tonight. Hudson clears his throat again, breaking me out of the weird trance I'm in. There won't be any late-night drinking or chatting tonight. It's going to end with me in my bed and him in his.

"Right, yeah," I whisper. "Good night."

He watches me walk to my room and waits until I shut the door before turning the lights off. I feel beat down while looking at the door.

What are we doing?

Why am I trying to play this game when he's withdrawn?

I don't go to the bathroom to change until I hear his door shut. I put on my pajamas and climb into bed with my phone in my hand to text Willow.

Me: How's everything going?

I'm not surprised when my phone beeps a few seconds later.

Willow: No updates. Results still don't look promising.

Me: I'm coming there tomorrow.

Willow: You don't have to do that.

Me: Yes, I do. You're my best friend.

Willow: Thank you. I love you.

Me: Love you more. Get some rest, girl.

I turn the ringer on high, in case she tries to call, and quickly fall asleep from exhaustion.

THE TEXT COMES before we board the flight to go back to LA.

Willow: Please tell me you haven't left to come here yet?

Me: No, we're scheduled to fly out in 20 minutes. What's up?

Willow: Don't.

My pulse spikes as I clasp my hand tighter around my phone in fear.

Me: What? Why? Did something happen to Brett?

I exit out of our text and try to call her, but it goes to voicemail.

Willow: Can't talk right now. Brett woke up.

I grin, jumping up and down while ignoring people's stares.

Me: That's great news! I'm so happy for you!

Isn't it? Because she sure doesn't seem happy about it. I would've expected a phone call from her beaming with excitement. Dread sinks into my stomach. Maybe he woke up, but that doesn't mean he's going to survive or be able to go back to his normal life.

Willow: It's crazy right now. Go home. Relax. I'll call you later and tell you everything. Love you.

Me: Love you. XO

I look over at Hudson, who's been giving me strange looks since my outburst of excitement. "False alarm. We're not going to Willow's."

"Is that good news or bad news?"

"I'm not exactly sure. Willow said he woke up, but there was no excitement, which is weird. It's like there's a void inside her right now, and I don't know what to do."

"Be patient with her. She's processing everything. Her world just tilted on its axis, and she's figuring out how to fix it."

"I guess you're right." This is unusual for Willow, but I'm going to give her time.

"So back to LA?"

"Back to LA."

CHAPTER FOURTEEN

Hudson

"WE MEET AGAIN," I say when I spot Stella stepping into the kitchen from the dark hallway. She's wearing something similar to what she had on the last time we were in this situation—lacy shorts and a tank top, sans bra.

I gulp, taking in the outline of her perky nipples underneath the tank.

Does she wear this shit every night?

Or is she still trying to break me down and convince me to give this casual sex offer a go?

"You can't sleep either?" I ask.

She's been slammed since we landed in LA this afternoon. We met with a friend of Willow's who's going to work part-time for Stella until she returns. The next stop was yoga class, which I thought would be a boring occasion, but surprisingly, I found it exciting. Seeing Stella in the downward dog position made my dick hard and showed me another one of her incredible traits. She's flexible as fuck, which is a plus in so many ways in the bedroom. We met her agent for dinner, and I listened to them talk about new show prospects.

A long day for Stella.

A boring as fuck one for me.

How did Dallas manage to go through this every day and not lose his mind?

"Unfortunately," she answers. "The stupid after-parties have my sleep schedule all out of whack." Her thick hair is pulled into two tight French braids that start at her crown and show off her high cheekbones.

I pat the chair next to me. "Good. Join the club."

Her full lips pinch together. "Good?"

"Yes, good, because not only can you keep me company, you can also make that weird, voodoo, puts you to sleep tea you swear by." I'm more excited about the company than the tea.

She throws her hands up in fake excitement. "Yay for me."

My eyes are trained to her as she moves around the kitchen to grab the teapot. I should offer to help, but I'm having too much fun watching her. Her top rises, giving me a glimpse of the bottom curves of her breasts, and my dick swells when she lifts up to grab the mugs from the top shelf of the cabinet.

I shift around in my seat, trying to talk my arousal down. She's here to make tea, not give me a boner. I promised myself to keep this professional, but the way she's swaying her hips while filling the pot is making me question my decision again.

I close my eyes and try to think of something else, but that only lasts a few seconds before they're wide open again, staring at her. I need to stop. I can't make our situation complicated because I'm going back to my normal life soon while she stays here in hers.

Normal life.

I laugh to myself. My life will never go back to the normal one I had in Blue Beech. There will be adjustments to make when I get home. I'm hoping another scandal has broken out that'll make people forget about Cameron fucking around on me. I don't want the stares of pity. I'm also going to have to pull in some of my anger toward Grady, so I don't punch him whenever we run into each other.

The perks of living in a small town.

I still prefer it to this LA shit. The traffic sucks. It takes hours to get anywhere, and the sidewalks are packed with women who look like they spent hours getting ready to get a kale smoothie. They had full faces of makeup *at the gym*.

"This might be completely out of left field," Stella starts to say, breaking me away from my thoughts. "But don't you think everything going on with us is weird?"

I have no idea what she's talking about. "What's weird?"

"Willow doesn't know if Brett is ever going to be the same. Dallas isn't sure how long he has left with Lucy. I feel like we have this cloud of death lingering over us, and we're waiting to see what tragedy happens first."

Thinking about losing Lucy is a punch to the gut. It won't only kill Dallas and Maven. It'll obliterate our entire family. She's been a constant in our lives for years. It's become an unnamed tradition that us Barnes boys tend to stay with our high school sweethearts and make a family. My parents did it. My grandparents did it. Dallas did it. Most of the other families in town do it. Those who do seem to be the happiest couples I know.

"I try not to look at it as we're waiting for Lucy to die," I say. "We're staying positive. Being a pessimist doesn't help the situation."

"I don't think I'm pessimistic. I'm just thinking about real life. It's never easy. Bad shit always happens. You'll never get through life unscathed."

Her answer hits a sensitive spot.

"Don't ever give up hope," I say. "You never know, both of them might make it through this standing tall. If there's one thing I've learned in my line of work, it's to never count anyone out until they're in a casket and someone is giving their eulogy. I've witnessed people lose their limbs. I've seen injuries so severe I thought they'd never see their families again, but you know what? They did. They survived because they were strong and badass fighters who knew they had an entire life ahead of them.

Sure, their lives may never be the same, but they're alive. They're waking up with their family. They're seeing the sunshine. Anything is possible. Without hope, you have nothing."

I close my eyes, recalling the memories and flashbacks of all the good and bad things I've seen throughout my career. Some of them I'll never get over. You don't forget seeing someone take their last breath.

My eyes open to find Stella at my side with a look on her face much different than when I shut them. Her dark eyes are glossy as she pulls out the chair next to mine and carefully takes my hand in hers. I flinch at first but don't pull away, which is what I should do.

"Sorry, what I said was completely insensitive," she whispers. "I'm sure that was hard on you, never knowing what would happen day by day, or what you were walking into."

She has no idea. No one does unless you've lived it. Pain is building in the back of my throat, in my heart, in my mind. Memories can be the scariest motherfuckers to haunt you at night.

She blows out a tortured breath before going on. "You're brave. I could never do anything like that. I want to thank you from the bottom of my heart for taking that job … and this one. No offense to your brother, but I've never felt safer than what I do with you." She holds our hands up and lightly brushes her soft lips against our connection.

It takes me a few seconds to regain control of myself. I don't want these wounds ripped open. I've tried my hardest to bury them, but somehow, Stella keeps digging deeper and deeper, forcing herself in. She's committed herself to discovering every component of me, whether I like it or not. This insane woman is getting closer and closer to my heart, and the harder I fight, the harder she does.

I clear my throat before bringing up our hands, pressing my lips to them just as she had. "Trust me, it's not easy. But I knew what I was getting into. I knew the possible outcome of going to another country and fighting. I think both of us knew the outcomes could've been bad when we chose our line of work."

She sighs when the teapot whistles through the air, and I place a hand on her arm to stop her from sliding out of her chair.

"Let me do it," I say.

I bring myself up when she nods and take the teapot off the heat. I've never made hot tea before, but it can't be that difficult.

"You're right about both of us knowing the risks in our jobs, but I'd say yours is much more intense. I get a lack of privacy, a few stalkers here and there, and people busting my ass about obligations. You get life or death, or possibly the loss of a limb. You do something so damn important, Hudson, and I wish they gave you more credit for it. I hate the way Tillie, Eli, all of them look as if you're beneath them, even though you're the real MVP."

I can't help but crack a smile, and she returns it in delight that she's hitting me where I never wanted to be cracked. She manages to bring out the light in me in even the worst times. Talking about this with someone is out of character for me. I've kept what I've seen, what I've gone through, to myself, allowing it to tear me apart from the inside.

Cameron grilled me with question after question when I got home from my first deployment. She wanted to know if I saw anyone die, if children actually walked the streets with homemade explosives strapped to their bodies, or if we spent our days doing nothing but playing around. She asked these questions as if I'd just gotten home from a banker's job.

I needed her to help me heal, but she only wanted to take me back down that road. She didn't understand. She only saw it as me shutting her out. I didn't want to release those internal demons on her or anyone else, so they stayed holed up inside me, burying themselves into my veins, where I'll live with them forever.

Stella gets up when she notices my hands start to shake while I pour the water into the mugs.

"Here," she says, taking it from me. She nudges her shoulder against mine. "I'm the tea master, so you better sit down and let the pro do her magic."

I give her a smile, one that's not forced, and do what she says. Stella is different. She cares. She respects me enough not to ask for the gruesome details. She's waiting for me to feel comfortable to release them on my own.

"Why did you join the military?" she asks, sliding my drink to me.

"You know, I'm not exactly sure. My grandfather served in Vietnam. My dad served. My family is big on tradition. One of my father's children needed to serve. I knew Dallas wasn't interested, and I'd never want to put that pressure on my sister, so I decided to take on the job. Another big push for me was what was happening in our country. I don't want to get political, but shit is fucked up. Innocent people have been dying for years."

She raises her cup. "I'll give an amen to that." She hops back on her chair and starts to sip on her drink, her full lips curving around the edge of the cup.

"Why did you decide to be Clementine?"

She squeals, grinning from ear to ear like I told her she won the lottery, and the mood has lifted. Tea splashes from my cup when she smacks me on the shoulder.

"Oh my god!"

I look around in confusion. "What?"

"You've been watching my show, haven't you?"

Fuck! I'm busted.

Stella had me too drowned in my feelings that I wasn't thinking about hiding that I've been secretly watching her show every night.

She smacks my shoulder again when I take a long drink without answering her. "Don't you dare lie to me."

I shake my head, my mouth still in my cup. "No. I've heard the name from Dallas."

"Oh, whatever, you've either been looking me up or watching. Which one is it?"

I set the cup down. There's nothing wrong with doing my research. "I was curious about who I was spending so much time with, so I watched a few episodes when I was bored."

She rests her hand against her chest and sways from side to side. "Hudson likes me; he really likes me," she sings out before pointing at me. "You shall never live this down. I'm beginning to think we might be getting closer than we thought we would. I have a feeling sex will be in our near future."

I decide to play along even though I'm thinking the same thing. "I must say Clementine grew out of her dorky phase into one fine as hell chick."

She laughs. "You are so lame."

CHAPTER FIFTEEN

Stella

MY PHONE RINGING interrupts our conversation. Willow's face pops up on the screen, and I try to answer so quickly I nearly drop it. As much as I want to continue this flirtatious conversation with Hudson, there's no way I'm missing her call. Something was wrong with her earlier, and I've been waiting to talk to her again. If she's calling this late, something is wrong.

I'm dreading whatever it is as I tap the Accept button.

"Hey girl," I answer, trying to sound upbeat.

"Hey," she says, sniffling.

Code Red. Code Red. Just what I thought.

"What's going on?" I rush out, my fake giddiness now disintegrated. I tuck the phone between my ear and shoulder.

There's a moment of silence, and I hold my breath for the news.

"Brett is awake and seems to be coherent," she finally tells me.

I exhale, confusion rushing through me. "That's great! It's a start, right?" I glance over to see Hudson's attention fixed on me.

"It is," she mutters. "I mean, I'm glad he's okay. He's recovering from a concussion, so he'll be in the hospital for a while. They're planning to perform facial reconstruction, but he's responsive and seems to have regained most of his memory."

Maybe her sniffles are sniffles of happiness.

"Good. I'm happy for you, Willow."

"He also decided he doesn't want to be with me anymore."

"What?" I yell louder than necessary.

Her sniffles turn into sobs. "He said his near-death experience woke him up." She scoffs. "*Literally.* Apparently, he wants to live his life and not be tied down. Settling is no longer an option for him." Her sobs turn into anger, and I wish I could wrap her in a tight hug and then take away Brett's cable TV in the hospital. "Disloyal son of a bitch. He's been *living his life* the way he's wanted for years. For fucking *years,* Stella! I stood by his cheating, no good ass every single damn day!"

I want to punch Brett in the balls and then elbow drop him for good measure. *How dare he do that to her?* Fucking asshole.

"Oh, and get this," she continues, huffing like she's exhausted every breath she has. "Some random chick showed up at the hospital the other day. His supposed side chick."

Damn side chicks. They always become a problem.

"I bet that went over well. Please tell me you're not calling me from jail and need to be bailed out for kicking her ass?"

"Hell no. She can have him. Let her see what a lying sack of scum he is."

"You deserve so much better. Everything will be okay, I promise. We'll find you a hot dude here, and you'll forget all about Brett's three-pump sex."

She sighs. "It's just a lot for me to take in, you know? I'm planning on coming back to work in a few days."

"Take your time. Do whatever you need to. Your job will be waiting for you whenever you're ready."

"Thanks. You seriously don't know how much I appreciate our friendship. I don't know what I'd do without you."

I wait to answer while she lets out a long yawn. "Get some sleep and call me in the morning, okay?"

"I will. Good night."

"Good night." I end the call and set down my phone before looking over at Hudson. "Brett is still awake and seems to have regained most of his memory."

He whistles. "Shit. You had me scared for a sec."

I cock my head to the side. "What? Why?"

"I thought the dude died, and you were comforting her by saying she can do better, and his dick game was weak."

"No, *so not* the case."

He smiles. "Then help me with my confusion, will ya?"

I don't want to repeat what Brett did because I'm so irate about it. My anger might force me to show up at the hospital and knock him upside the head with a frying pan. Maybe he needs to suffer another concussion so he can wake up from the next one with more sense.

"He woke up and decided to dump her ass," I tell him, snarling my lip.

He scowls. "You're shitting me?"

I shake my head. "I wish I was. Douchebag wants to spread his wings like a pigeon and spread his bullshit to more of the female population."

Hudson sips his tea. "Sounds like a good man."

"Yep, even better news is that the chick he's been cheating with showed up at the hospital devastated."

He winces, his expression switching from resentment to pure hatred. He looks like he wants to be the next one in line to elbow drop Brett.

"I despise cheaters," he hisses. "They disgust me. Willow deserves better."

I nod in agreement. "It's not the first time he's been caught cheating. It happens all the time, and then he begs her to stay with him while giving some bullshit speech that he'll change. For some reason, Willow always falls for it. I pray it doesn't happen again."

His jaw muscles clench. "They never change. Once a cheater, always a cheater. Period."

"I … I don't think that's necessarily true," I stutter out. "People make mistakes and learn from them all the time."

This is about his ex, and I hate that he's so angry about it. He's still in love with her. That's the reason for a reaction like that.

"Cheating isn't a mistake. It's unforgivable in my book. It breaks the bond of trust, and if I can't trust you, I can't be with you. It's not that difficult for someone to take a step back and realize that cheating on someone will tear them apart in every way possible. Make them feel like they're not good enough."

I gulp. This night had been going so well. He catches onto my uneasiness and snaps out of his frustration, his face apologetic.

"Shit, I'm sorry," he says. "You don't want to hear me whine about this shit. I shouldn't have acted like that." He finishes his tea. "It's probably time we get to bed." This seems to be a constant with him. We get somewhere, then he walks away. "Good night, Stella. Sleep well."

"Good night," I whisper.

I wait until I hear his bedroom door close before grabbing my phone and opening Instagram. I type Hudson's name, but my search comes up empty. I type Dallas's name next.

Jackpot.

There's nothing more satisfying than finding the person you want to stalk's profile is public.

Creeping here I come.

I scroll through his photos. Most of them are of him with Maven and Lucy. I spot the most recent one with Hudson. They're at his welcome home party. Hudson looks happy, a beer in his hand, and his arms around his brother and a short, dark-haired woman. I narrow my eyes at her but relax when I notice she's tagged in the caption as Lauren Barnes, their sister.

I proceed with my stalking until I'm well into weirdo territory and find one with Dallas, Lucy, Hudson, and a stunning blonde. I click on it and study the picture. Everyone is smiling, and she's tucked into Hudson's side, his arm around her.

It has to be the ex-girlfriend.

And she looks exactly like a woman I imagine Hudson with. Her hair is naturally blond and down in loose, effortless waves, and she's wearing cut-off shorts and a tee showing plenty of cleavage. The photo proves how deep Hudson loved her. There's a different light in his eyes than he has now.

I click on her tagged username to see more pictures of her and maybe the ex-best friend. It'd be hard finding someone better looking than Hudson. Someone who could compete with him.

Did she keep pictures of her and Hudson up or delete them?

Unfortunately, her profile is private.

Loser.

The only way I can advance further into my operation stalk Hudson mission is if I request to follow her, which will make me look like an insane person.

Game over for me.

I frown, pissed at my defeat, and decide to go to bed with Hudson on my mind.

CHAPTER SIXTEEN

Hudson

I ACTED like a douche lord in the kitchen.

I never meant to expose myself like that to Stella.

I'm not in love with Cameron anymore. I don't want her back. Once a cheater, you're always a fucking cheater in my playbook. What triggered my anger wasn't losing her. It was the lies and deception. I would've given my life for Cameron, sacrificed everything I had to make sure she was safe and happy, only to find out she'd turned her back on me when times got just *slightly* tough.

She should've come to me, told me she didn't want that life, and I would've gladly let her off the hook.

It only proves that pursuing a relationship with a friend you've known your entire life is a bad idea, which is why I'm taking a hiatus from dating. Whether I'm taking a break from fucking is still yet to be determined because my mind—my dick—can't stop thinking about dipping into some sweet pussy.

It's been too long since I've been intimate with a woman, and there's nothing more on your mind than getting laid when you come home from a long deployment. My problem is that my pussy-deprived mind is wrapped around tasting my new employer.

I snatch my laptop from the desk and power it up to start the second season of Stella's show. I shake my head at my stupidity of letting it slip that I've been watching it, but the excitement in her eyes told me she liked it. She's made it clear she's all in. She's mine temporarily if I make the move, and each passing minute with her is pushing me closer in her direction.

I blow out a breath.

I can't believe I'm about to say this.

"I'm bound to screw Stella Mendes," I whisper into the emptiness of my room. "And God help me, I think I'm falling for her."

"MORNING."

Stella's greeting is wrapped around a yawn. Her ebony hair is down and wild with tangles—my favorite look on her. I love seeing her unpolished, raw, untamed.

She's wearing different pajamas than she wore last night. The dark silk nearly blends in with her hair, and the tank is cut so low I'm sure I'll get a view of her nipples if she leans down far enough.

That'd be a good way to start the morning.

I lick my lips. *Fuck.* I need to smack some sense into myself with the whisk in my hand, but instead, I settle it on the side of the bowl and rub my hands over my sweats.

"Adulting fuel?" I ask, turning around to make her a cup of coffee without waiting for her response.

She yawns again. "Is that even a question?"

I pour her a cup, adding two teaspoons of sugar and a splash of coconut milk. I somehow have her coffee preference down, which further proves that I'm being an idiot and getting too close. I've even started making my coffee the same way. I never had coconut milk before coming here, but it's not too bad.

"Thanks," she says when I hand her the mug. She stands on her tiptoes to see what I'm doing. "You're making breakfast?"

I shrug. "I figured why not? You said your chef is on vacation, and I'm starving. It would've been rude for me to only make enough for one."

I grew up with a mother that always cooked enough to feed a football team. We seemed to constantly have a houseful of people—cousins, girlfriends, neighbors. People showed up, and we fed them.

"Always the gentleman," she says with a light laugh. "You need any help?"

I shake my head before tipping it toward the island. "Sit down and enjoy your coffee. You might be the master tea-maker, but I'm the breakfast expert."

She gives me a skeptic look. "Do you actually know how to cook? Or do I need to collect my valuables before you burn my house down?" She drags out a chair from underneath the island and sits.

"Sure do. When I was younger, my parents made us do the outside and inside chores, so we'd be a jack-of-all-trades. I can change your tire and then come home and bake you a scrumptious as fuck pecan pie."

She leans forward to settle an elbow on the counter, her chin resting in her cupped palm. "A jack-of-all-trades, huh? I like it. You fix shit, shoot shit, and cook shit."

I snap my fingers. "I think I'll make that my next pickup line."

"I expect royalties when it's successful and you get laid." She pauses, a smile growing. "Unless it's with me. I'll let you have a free pass then."

"You better quit trying to fuck me before I burn your breakfast."

"Eh, I wouldn't mind. To be honest, I've had my fair share of burnt food. Cooking is not one of my strong suits."

My shoulders relax now that she's changed the subject and isn't going to keep exciting my dick.

"Even when I try, I always seem to mess something up." She leans back, her manicured fingers wrapping around the handle of the mug, and keeps her eyes glued to me while I move around and do my thing. "But I have to say, I enjoy watching you in my kitchen. There's something sexy about a man putting in the effort to do something like this instead of calling room service or texting his chef what my favorite meal is."

"That's good to know." I can't believe she's never had a dude cook for her.

"*Although,* if you take your shirt off, it'll be even sexier." She grins, a flush creeping up her cheeks.

I hold up the whisk, batter dripping from it while trying to keep a straight face. "You keep trying to get me naked, I might have to file a sexual harassment charge against you."

She blows out a dramatic breath. "Why are you making it such a challenge? I thought all men like to get laid, especially when a woman is putting a no-strings-attached clause on the table. I feel like this should be the other way around."

"You might want to change your taste in men, Hollywood. Not all of us only care about getting our dicks wet. I think it would freak the hell out of you if I kept begging you to jump on my dick. I'd be like Eli's creepy bodyguard."

She shudders. "True story, but trust me, I wouldn't mind it from you." She licks her lips. "In fact, I'd encourage it."

"I'll keep that in mind."

"That's what you keep saying," she mutters. "Cock block."

I shake my head, laughing, and start to dip the bread in the batter.

"What's on the menu?"

"French toast and scrambled eggs."

"Sounds good."

She starts telling me stories of her cooking fails while I finish up our food. I hand her a plate, grab all the necessities for the meal, and pour her another cup of coffee.

She looks from my plate to my stomach and then to my plate again when I sit down next to her. "Question, how do you eat like this and look like *that?*"

"I work out," I answer, grabbing the sugar-free syrup, which is all she has, and pour it onto my plate. I do it to hers next. "Although, I've been slacking on it since I've been here. Your gym consists of mostly cardio machines."

I wait for her to take the first bite, dying to see her reaction, and grin when she does.

She chews, swallows her bite down, and then stabs at her next one with a fork. "This is incredible. I wasn't expecting it to be this good."

We dig in, our conversation sparse as we stuff our faces, and she helps me clean up when we're finished. She's wiping her hands on a dish towel when she looks over at me with a grin. I know I'm in trouble.

"Back to the working out conversation," she says. "I have news that'll brighten your day."

I arch a brow. "Oh, really?"

"My yoga instructor is coming over for a morning session. Do it with me. We can burn off all those delicious carbs we just devoured."

Yoga?

I snort. "Thanks, but I'll have to pass on that."

She doesn't seem fazed by my dismissal. "Have you ever even tried it before?"

"Nope, and never plan to. Twisting myself into pretzel positions doesn't seem like a good time to me or my junk."

"It's not only twisting yourself into pretzel positions. Don't knock something until you try it. Plus, you said you've been slacking on your workouts."

I shake my head. "Still not happening."

She pouts her lips. "*Please,* for me."

I shake my head again.

"You're doing it, so get dressed, soldier. You're about to have your first yoga lesson."

I throw my head back, knowing damn well I'm about to cave. "How do I keep letting you talk me into shit I'd never do?"

She laughs and slaps my stomach as she walks by. "It'll be fun. I promise."

"If not, you better make it up to me," I yell to her back while getting a good view of her ass.

She whips back around. "I have no problem with that. I'm up for anything."

"*I'll* keep that in mind." We're playing a dangerous game.

She's laughing as she disappears into the foyer. I go to my room to change and grab my phone.

Me: What the hell does a dude wear to yoga?

Stella: It's nude yoga, so you don't have to worry about attire.

Me: You and your instructor are going to piss yourself when I show up in my birthday suit.

Stella: I dare you to do it.

Fucking with me seems to be her new favorite hobby. Stella will be the death of my morals. My momma will have a coronary if she sees me in some tabloid love triangle. People will think I'm the scum of the earth for messing with another man's woman, and I'll never be able to tell my truth because Stella will hate me if I let her secret out.

Operation Keep My Dick In My Pants is now in order.

I have a feeling I'm going to fail.

My phone rings. I snatch it up from the bed and balance it on my shoulder as I pull my shorts up.

"Hello?" I answer.

"How are things going?" Dallas asks.

"Good." I pause, debating with myself on whether to tell him. "About to have yoga class."

He laughs for a good thirty seconds. "You're shitting me?"

I stay quiet.

"You're doing yoga now?"

"No, asshat. I'm escorting Stella to yoga," I lie.

"Bullshit. You're going to climb up on that mat and Namaste the fuck out of your problems. Next time I see you, you'll be eating seaweed and hugging trees."

"Fuck off, what can I help you with?"

"Doing my daily check-in to see where your head is, and if you're done being a grumpy bastard yet."

"I think you know I'll always be a grumpy bastard, but it's getting better." That's an understatement. "It does get dull when I'm following her around doing mundane shit. How did you manage to do this for so long?"

"I don't know. I guess I got used to it. You will, too."

"No, I won't. I'm only here temporarily, remember?"

"I stand corrected. Get your yoga on and text me later. Maven is insisting I have a tea party with her."

"You're giving me shit about yoga when you're about to have drinks with stuffed animals?"

"The perks of having a kid, man."

I hang up and open my suitcase for a shirt. I haven't unpacked because *I'm not staying long.*

CHAPTER SEVENTEEN

Stella

HUDSON DOESN'T SHOW up naked to yoga, much to my dismay.

However, he does show, which gives me some optimism.

Today's yoga session will be interesting.

He might be wearing clothes, but there's not much to them. I slowly lick my lips, taking him in as he comes farther into the kitchen wearing athletic shorts that hang low on his hips and a T-shirt with the sleeves cut off that gives me the perfect view of his firm forearms and chiseled triceps.

I smile, lamely feeling special that I've convinced such a macho man to do this with me. He's beginning to surprise me more with every minute we spend together. I can feel him dragging me into his world, and I have a nervous feeling that if I get swept up, I'll never want to let go.

It's the calm before the storm.

It's going to happen, and I don't know how bad the devastation will be when it ends.

His mind is like a mystery book I want to read every page of.

Has he changed his opinion about me?

Does he think I'm a creep for hitting on him all the time?

Does he consider it sexual harassment?

Is he going to sue my ass because I want to get a piece of his?

His unpredictability is killing me.

It's also what's drawing me to him.

He's different.

He hasn't tried to sleep with me, even when I handed him my vagina on a silver platter. He doesn't only have a conversation with me in hopes it ends with my lips around his cock. The roles are reversed from anything I've ever experienced.

I'm the chaser this time, the beggar, the one who's throwing her panties at him and insisting he fuck me sideways … long ways … hell, any way, for that matter.

I want him. His cock. His tongue. His fingers. His touch.

Anything he's willing to give.

Just as long as it's *him.*

I'm a strong supporter of orgasms. I was always open to trying new things with Knox. We did the whole foreplay fun, experimented with our tongues and fingers for over a year before finally losing our virginities to each other.

What's surprising me is that I've never coveted someone's touch so powerfully before as I do with Hudson. I've never felt myself grow wet between my legs or had my heart rage out of control when I'm at the receiving end of someone's smile.

But I do with him.

I jump when the doorbell rings, and it takes away the opportunity for me to drill him on why he has clothes on. I'm wondering when I became this sex-crazed maniac as I spin around on my heels to answer the door and let Yolanda in.

"Good morning, sunshine," she sings out in her Dutch accent, strutting in with her yoga mat strapped around her shoulder. She gives me a peck on each cheek. "I saw the new movie. *Fabulous!* Absolutely fabulous."

Yolanda is the best yoga instructor in LA. She makes a killing off house calls because she's like some yogi expert. I met her when I attended one of her sessions at a friend's home about a year ago and was instantly hooked. I was still healing from my breakup with Knox and felt like a sad loser. She turned my depression into something positive. I walked out with a different perspective on life and hired her to come over two days a week when I'm in the city.

"Thank you," I say, leading her into the house.

"Are we doing in or out?" she asks.

"The weather is perfect, so let's go outside."

"I hoped you'd say that. Your view is one of my favorites. If you ever need someone to house-sit, I'm your girl."

"My bodyguard is also going to join us today."

Hudson steps forward at the mention of him when we reach the kitchen. "I'm a newbie," he says, shooting her a polite grin. "Be easy on me."

He winks, and I swear to God, Yolanda almost melts right in front of us. Let's add charmer to the list of Hudson's hot qualities.

"Of course," Yolanda answers. "What made you decide to join us?"

"It wasn't my idea." He points at me. "This one is hard to say no to."

Yolanda looks back at me with an arched brow and what I'm certain is a *you're so fucking him* look.

If only.

I open the French doors leading outside and walk outside to the patio by the pool in my backyard. I bought this house after my breakup with Knox. It was the first time I'd ever been on my own. I went from living with my mom to moving straight in with him when I turned eighteen. It's exciting to have something that only belonged to me. Having my own home gives me a sense of pride.

The backyard is what made me fall in love with the property. I put in an offer the same day as the showing. The infinity pool stretches out to the hills, plus a firepit and a hot tub and enough seating to entertain fifty people even though I've only had company a few times.

Yolanda strips off her shirt, showing off her black sports bra and a six-pack I'd kill for, and sets her mat down on the concrete. She's in her late forties but has the body of a woman my age.

I peek down at my stomach. It's flat, but my hips have a little too much *handle* in the love handle department. I'm not skinny, but I wouldn't say I'm overweight. I like to refer to myself as full of tits and ass. I inherited my mother's wide hips and large bust, but I try to keep my body in as good as shape as I can. That doesn't mean I'll turn down tacos.

I bend down to set my mat on the ground and hand Hudson my extra one.

He holds it up, raising a brow. "Pink?"

I smirk. "It brings out the color in your eyes."

He chuckles. "Good to know."

Yolanda starts us out in child's pose when we get ourselves situated and begins her mantra.

WE'RE thirty minutes into yoga, and I'm not feeling my Zen self, per usual. I'm not following along with any of Yolanda's instructions … because I'm turned on.

She directs us to go into downward facing dog, but I'm only catching onto bits and pieces of what she's saying. Her words are like background noise while I focus all my attention on Hudson, who is now shirtless and following Yolanda's orders.

He goes into the pose, his back arched and ass sticking up in the air, and I do the same. Sweat drips off his forehead and chest.

Is it gross that I want to wipe him clean with my tongue?

I shake my head in a failed attempt to focus on the task of getting my shit together, but my knees are trembling. My elbows are wobbly. I clench my fingers and toes, certain I'm about to fail at this pose even though I've done it dozens of times.

Think about peaceful shit, for God's sake.

You're in fucking yoga class.

Buddha.

Gandhi.

Not Hudson's penis.

Penis is not Zen.

No Zen is flowing through me right now.

No *Namaste bitches,* here.

I peel my attention away from Hudson when Yolanda gets up to adjust his pose. He glances over at me, and we make eye contact as he shoots me a playful grin that nearly causes me to fall. Yolanda comes my way next, most likely confused about why I'm fumbling around like a two-year-old who finally discovered she has legs.

My eyes don't leave his as Yolanda quickly corrects me and then goes back to her mat. Hudson's intense gaze impales mine, his rustic honey eyes drinking me in, and I can't look away. This only ratifies that I'm not the only one feeling this connection, this chemistry sparking between us.

Our connection is snapped a few minutes later when Yolanda has us move into the last position, and we finish our session.

Hudson stands and starts picking up our mats while I walk Yolanda to the front door, my feet slowly sliding along the travertine tile. A part of me wants to push her out of my house and race over to Hudson. The other part of me wants to beg her to stay because I don't know what's going to happen when she leaves.

She turns around and hugs me. "He seems like a keeper, that one."

"He's only my bodyguard," I say, trying to convince us both. "Nothing more."

"Nothing more *yet*, but I have a feeling there will be. I'm an instructor, which means I'm trained to watch. I saw the chemistry bleeding between you two. A spark that wants its final connection. The way your expressions altered while watching each other move into the next pose told me everything I need to know. There will be more. I can promise you that."

She gives me a final wave and disappears out the door.

I sigh. I'm usually relaxed when she leaves, but that's not the case today.

I'm on edge.

Is yoga supposed to trigger sexual arousal?

It brings out pheromones, dopamine, and all that good stuff, right?

It's never happened before, but I've also never done it with Hudson.

Never done it with *a shirtless and sweaty* Hudson.

I find him in the kitchen. He has his shirt back on and is pulling out two bottles of water from the fridge. I smile when he hands one to me.

"What did you think?" I ask, leaning against the island. "Are you ready to be the next yoga enthusiast?"

He wipes his forehead with the back of his arm. "It wasn't that bad."

I snort.

"Fine, it's not exactly my preferred type of exercise."

I lift my chin slightly. "What is your preferred type of exercise?"

"High-intensity shit. Loud music. Definitely no fucking chanting involved."

His answer doesn't surprise me.

"There has to be something you liked about it."

He smiles. "You're right. I enjoyed watching you."

Whoa. I almost drop my water.

I was on course to settle my hormones, but that response charges them back with the accelerator on high.

I straighten my stance, feeling brave. "What a coincidence. I enjoyed watching you."

A moment of silence passes through the air as we stare at each other. His breathing quickens, his chest moving in and out rapidly, and I prepare myself for rejection again.

"Fuck it," he mutters.

I'm too stunned to move as I watch him advance around the island with determination on his face. He cups the back of my neck and pulls me to him, our lips meeting, and nearly knocks the air from my lungs. My water bottle falls to the floor.

His lips are softer than I imagined. I'd watched him, studied the way he talked, laughed, and even grimaced, and wondered how they'd feel against mine if he ever gave in to temptation. He yanks me closer, his free arm curving around my waist, and gives me what I've been begging for.

Our breathing collides when his tongue slides against mine, and I stand on my tiptoes to better meet his mouth. His scruff brushes over my cheek, something I've never experienced before. Most men I've kissed have been clean-shaven. I'm positive I'll have beard burn on my cheek tomorrow and am hoping it'll also be between my legs.

My heart plummets when he pulls away. I squeeze my eyes shut, expecting him to stop, but he cradles my cheeks in his palms. I slowly open my eyes.

I'm panting. He's panting.

My back straightens while he holds me in place, and I wait for him to make the next move. It's taking forever.

"Look at me, Stella," he demands.

I stare into his eyes as he looks at me with a tenderness I've never experienced before.

He lowers his voice. "You're beautiful." He traces my lips with his finger. "You've probably been told that a million times, but there's no superior word to describe you."

It's my turn to initiate a kiss.

This time, we kiss with no hesitancy.

I suck on the tip of his tongue and savor the taste of him.

He picks me up, and I wrap my legs around his waist when he carries me to the living room. My hands shake when he carefully deposits me on the couch. Excitement shoots through me when he drops to his knees and tugs on my yoga pants. I lift my legs, assisting him in getting the job done faster, and my lungs are burning from breathing so hard.

My pants get tossed to the side, and he settles between my legs.

This isn't a fair fight.

He's calling the shots.

And surprisingly, I have no problem with it.

"Fuck, these are sexy," he says, tracing the edge of my panties where the lace meets my thigh. I throb between my legs when he skates his finger back and forth torturously. I push my hips up, a silent plea for more, and he takes the hint by hooking his fingers through the sides of my panties and tears them down my legs.

"Is this what you want?" he asks. "Tell me this is what you want."

Did he get fucking dementia?

I've been begging for this.

I decide against telling him that. Throwing around attitude when a man you're sure knows what he's doing is about to pleasure you isn't a smart idea.

"It's everything I want," I answer. "You're everything I want, Hudson."

My truth shocks the shit out of us both.

It also excites him.

His fingers dig into my hips, and he pulls me closer to his mouth. My legs are spread wide before he runs his tongue deep inside me.

The first lick has me craving more.

He uses the tip of his tongue to play with my clit and then shoves a finger deep inside me. My back arches as I moan, and he pumps his finger in and out of me, his tongue still working on driving me wild.

Fucking hell!

His tongue has me writing my vows.

Imagine what he can do with his cock.

He mercilessly adds another finger. I buck against his touch, my pussy walls tightening around his fingers like a glove, and he doesn't stop until I'm writhing against the couch while pleasure explodes through me.

"Let go, Stella," he says. "Let me see you get off."

I come alive and cry out as my orgasm shakes through me while he tells me how sexy I look. My legs shake as I sink my nails into the throw pillow next to me and try to catch my breath.

"Fuck me now," I order, coming down from the history-making orgasm but still not fulfilled.

He gives me one last lick before pulling away. I stare at him nervously while waiting for his next move. His jaw is tight, and he looks at me like he's on the edge of losing control. My head is level with his waist when he stands, and I take in the view of his erection showing through his shorts.

It would be so easy to reach out and touch him, but I resist. I need that same validation he wanted from me. I want him to tell me he's craving to have me as much as I am him.

He makes eye contact and peels off his shirt. I take in the sight of his chest and even though I've seen it before, it doesn't fail to turn me on.

"Drop them," I demand, my voice filled with authority.

He drops his shorts, and my pulse races.

His perfect cock twitches in front of me. It's swollen, thick, and I moan at the thought of how amazing it will feel sliding inside me. He doesn't waste another second before grabbing his erection at the base, and we both take a deep breath when he situates himself at my entrance.

I throw my head back when he slowly inserts the head.

Then I look back at him at the feel of him pulling away.

No! Why?

"Fuck," he hisses. "I don't have a condom."

Neither do I.

Since I was under the impression I wouldn't need them, I stupidly didn't bother restocking when I ran out.

"I'm on the pill," I blurt out, most likely sounding desperate.

Don't stop.

Don't walk away from this.

"I don't fuck without a condom." He scrubs a hand over his face and takes a step back.

A step that stomps on my heart.

I put my hands between my legs to cover myself and suddenly feel too exposed. "You never screwed your ex-fiancé without a condom?"

He snatches my pants from the floor and hands them to me before putting his shirt on. "Yes, on occasions."

"So, *you do* fuck without a condom." I don't know why I feel like this is a sucker punch to the stomach.

"I've never had sex with a stranger without a condom."

He's never had sex with a stranger, period. His insult makes me feel dirty in a way. Even though he's being responsible, I'm not a *stranger*. I'm not some chick he met in the club ten minutes ago.

"But you'll lick their vagina?" I argue.

He clenches his jaw. "Please don't take it the wrong way, Stella. It's not a diss to you."

How do I handle this situation?

What do I do now?

Do I shake his hand, thank him for his time, and then chat about the weather?

Storm Stella is about to roll through and punch him in the balls.

"Are you scared that you'll catch something from me?"

He winces. "Fuck no."

"Then what? Do you still have a problem with my so-called fake hooking?"

"No," he grits out. "Don't fucking put words in my mouth."

"Then correct me where I'm wrong."

My phone rings, and I roughly pull my pants up and rush into the kitchen to hide my embarrassment.

My shame.

My fucking stupidity.

I hold up my phone. "That's my reminder alarm. We have to go to my audition."

Yay. I get to spend an entire car ride with him.

He steps my way, putting his palms out in front of him. "Stella, please."

"Just stop, okay?"

Out of all people, why did I attempt to screw my bodyguard?

The guy who has to follow me and be around at all times.

CHAPTER EIGHTEEN

Hudson

I SIT down on the edge of my bed and rub my sweaty forehead.

My cock is still as hard as a rock.

Stella said she was going to change and rushed out of the room like she couldn't stand to look at me for a second longer.

Not that I can blame her.

I'm a disgrace to men right now.

A disgrace to everything I stand for.

I was careless and only thinking with my dick, not about what would happen if we crossed that line.

So much for keeping our relationship professional.

The way I ate her pussy was far from that.

The hunger to taste her everywhere was tormenting me, and I couldn't hold back any longer. Stopping us from having sex was one of the hardest decisions I've had to make.

I'm an asshole. I used the same mouth I pleasured her with to insult her. The words came out wrong. I could barely stutter out a decent excuse, and then she accused me of being scared she'd give me a damn STD.

That's not what stopped me.

Shit can happen, and birth control doesn't always work. Dallas and Lucy thought they were careful and then got pregnant with Maven. I gulp. Cameron got pregnant when she was on the pill two years ago. Even though we hadn't planned it, we were excited. Then we lost the baby ten weeks later. I never want to feel grief that hard again.

It nearly killed us.

We spent months mourning our loss, and the fear of another miscarriage put stress on us.

Maybe that's what killed our relationship.

"I'M SORRY," I say when Stella gets into the SUV.

Jim has a few days off, so I've been driving her around.

I keep the keys in my hand. We're not leaving until she hears me out.

"What I said came out wrong," I continue. "I'm not experienced with this shit."

She shakes her head without looking at me.

"Say something, *please.* I feel like a fucking piece of shit."

She glares at me. "You had a girlfriend for nearly a decade. You're experienced. Hell, you're more experienced than men who have screwed dozens of women because you were there for your girlfriend not only physically but also emotionally." She shakes her head. "I get it. I'm not your type. You don't see me *for me*. You made that clear from day one."

"I'll admit I was wrong for judging you in the beginning, but I'm fighting with myself on what to do here. I explained why taking that step for us wasn't a good idea. I'm moving in two months. We'll never be able to have a relationship."

She crosses her arms. "Why does it have to be a relationship? Why can't we try something casual?"

"Do you think we can honestly do that? Only sex?"

Maybe she can, but I can't.

I've never been able to separate my feelings from sex because I've never had to.

"I don't know, but I feel like we need to do something. I can't stop wanting more with you. Why can't we try? If it doesn't work out, you can walk away without giving me a reason. I won't ask any questions."

Casual sex has never interested me.

She frowns when I shove the keys into the ignition.

"We should get going," I say. "Don't want you to be late."

"You are the most confusing person on this fucking planet," she groans.

She stays on her phone while I follow the GPS instructions. My thoughts roam with every passing mile. Maybe I should give casual sex a try.

I was monogamous for years. That didn't work out.

Maybe it's time for a change.

We can both use each other.

CHAPTER NINETEEN

Stella

I'M FORCING a fake smile while staring at the script in my hand.

I did my makeup and rode thirty minutes in traffic hell for this?

I hate it.

The character sucks.

The storyline sucks.

And the cherry on top is that my management company loves it and wants me to take it as my next gig.

Fuck my life.

Margot, the next damsel in distress, is not the role for me.

I took the role with my last movie to get my feet wet in the industry like my team advised, but I refuse to continue playing the naïve woman needing a man supporting her to survive. That's not the career path I want.

This chick stalks—*yes, freaking stalks*—a man she met in a coffee shop because he resembles her ex-boyfriend. She then proceeds to ruin his fiancé's life in order to get his attention, and they fall in love in the end.

This is a love story?

I can't play the role of a desperate and obsessed psychopath.

Sure, I've been crushing on Hudson since he moved in and

have made sexual advances like a cat in heat, but I'm not standing over his bed at night and watching him sleep. I stupidly didn't do my homework and read the script before coming, but I was too busy. Not to mention, my management team made it sound mandatory.

"Stella."

The feminine voice startles me, and I look up at the producer and casting director as they stare at me in question.

"Huh?" I ask.

"I asked if Eli will have an issue with you having another man as a love interest," she answers with annoyance. "Some men don't want their girlfriends making out with other men."

I bite back my smart-ass comment for the sake of my career. Maybe if I tell her Eli is a possessive freak who will cut my toes off if I kiss someone else, they won't give me the role, and management won't be up my ass about it.

"Uh, no," I mutter. "He knows how the industry works. We both do."

Yes, I'm a chickenshit. Sue me.

She stacks her papers and presses them against the table. "Perfect. We'll be in touch."

I deliver another forced smile and exit the room, passing a row of other women auditioning to be Margot The Maniac.

Hudson jumps up from his chair when he sees me, and I follow him outside to the SUV. He's still on my shit list. I'm humiliated by what happened. I was there, completely bared to him, and he walked away as if it was nothing. If he thought his bullshit apology in the car would make it better, he's stupid.

"How did it go?" he questions, turning on the car.

I cross my arms and sulk in my seat. "I don't want to talk about it."

"You didn't get it?"

"I probably did."

"Then why does it look like someone told you your dog died?"

"Because I'm having a pretty shitty day, thanks in large part to you." I hold two fingers inches apart from each other. "We were *this* close to having sex." I stretch them out, emphasizing my aggravation. "Not only did I lose the opportunity to possibly have the best sex of my life because the orgasm-giver turned out to be a complete a-hole, I then had to leave and audition for the stupidest role in the world."

"Look, I'm sorry. What I said wasn't what I meant, and I'll continue telling you that until you forgive me. I can get annoying as fuck, too, trust me."

"If that's your plan to make me feel better, it sucks ass."

"Shit." He pinches the bridge of his nose, shaking his head. "I acted like an idiot. Not for the whole condom situation, but for how I treated you." He signals back and forth between us. "You and I both know it's not going to end well if we take this step."

"You didn't even give it a chance."

"I know, and I'm sorry. So damn sorry. I promise I'll make it up to you."

His apology doesn't help. The urge to call him a coward is hanging on the tip of my tongue, but it's no use. His mind was made up about me from the moment he landed at LAX.

I cross my arms. "Fine, and I'm going to keep you to that, by the way."

"I know I'm in the wrong, but can you at least give me credit for eating your pussy until you fell apart on my tongue?" His tone changes from apologetic to cocky.

He does have a point.

He didn't exactly leave me high and dry.

More along the lines of panting and soaked.

I sigh, not willing to let him win yet. "What orgasm? I was faking it so you wouldn't feel bad."

He throws his head back. "Oh Hollywood, you may be an actress, but that wasn't acting."

I give him a dirty look. "Whatever." My stomach growls. "I

know you like to withhold me from life's necessities and all, but can you at least feed me? I've already been starved of another orgasm from you."

He grins. "A life necessity, huh?"

I can't hold back my laughter any longer.

"There's that smile."

My smile collapses into a frown. "Don't. I'm still fucking livid at you."

He chuckles, aware he's winning this round. "Where to?"

I give him directions to my favorite sushi joint a few miles away. I'm letting him off the hook too easily, but he's right. Sex without a condom would have been reckless.

I have no idea what's going on in his downstairs area. I mean, I don't think he has anything, but you never know. At least one of us was thinking rationally.

I can't get pregnant. My head aches at the thought of it. I can barely take care of myself, let alone be responsible for another human. I have someone who schedules my manicures, for Christ's sake.

He pulls up to the curb in front of the restaurant and unbuckles his seat belt. "Do you want me to grab you takeout, or are you meeting someone and want me to wait out here?"

"Give the keys to the valet," I direct him. "We're dining in."

"We're?"

I nod when he gestures back and forth between the two of us to clarify.

"Not a good idea, Hollywood."

"Am I that embarrassing to be around?"

"Yes. Look at you, all perfect and sexy. I'll get made fun of for days if I hang out with such a creature."

I unbuckle my seat belt and push his side. "Come on. I'm starving, and my sushi craving is killing me with every second we're having this ridiculous conversation."

He doesn't move. "Did you say sushi?"

"Sure did."

He shakes his head. "Nuh-uh, I don't eat that raw fish, seaweed shit."

"Who doesn't eat sushi?"

"Me, that's who. I already let you convince me to spend my morning twisting my limbs into positions that my balls will never forgive me for. I draw the line at eating that shit. I like my fish fried, baked, anything but raw."

I roll my eyes but laugh. "Too bad. I'm not eating alone."

I open my door and jump out without waiting for his response. He curses under his breath as he joins me and hands the valet the keys.

"Pain in my ass," he grumbles while opening the door for me.

"Payback's a bitch."

"YOU SURE THEY don't have burgers here?" Hudson asks, turning the menu front to back a few times as though he's missing something. "There's a hidden menu you don't want me to see, isn't there?"

"Try the damn sushi and quit being a diva. I'm sure you've eaten worse."

"I absolutely have, but not when I've had the choice."

"How about you try this, and I'll let you choose dinner, deal?"

He smirks. "You plan to share another meal with me?"

I look down in an attempt to hide my smile. "Possibly." *I do! I do!*

He slides his menu to me from across the table. "Order me whatever you're having."

When the waiter brings our sushi, I make him take the first bite. Hudson stares at it with a scrunched-up nose and slowly picks up the chopsticks. He pinches the chopsticks together, picks up a roll, and examines it before shoving the sushi in his mouth.

"Admit it," I say when he starts chewing. "It's not bad."

"Fine," he groans, swallowing it down. "You win."

I clap my hands and squeal.

"Settle down. I'm not saying I want to eat it every day of my life."

With a smile, I grab my chopsticks and dig in. That's when they walk in, and I nearly choke on my food. Hudson's attention shoots to me in worry while I force myself to swallow down my bite.

"Just when I thought the humiliation of today couldn't get worse," I mutter, narrowing my eyes on the movement behind him. My stomach churns when the couple sits down at a table on the other side of the room.

Hudson turns around to see what's caught my attention. "I'd like to think you had a pretty good start to the day." He shifts back around. "Who's the dude?"

I haven't seen Knox in months, nor have I wanted to. His hair is grown out, and he's gained weight, but he looks happy. The smile on his face is a reminder of when we were young and in love—before the industry beat us up.

His new girlfriend is with him. I recognize her from the tabloids and have been questioned about her in interviews, when people ask for my autograph, or when the paparazzi just want to be assholes.

Everyone wants to know what I think about the woman who allegedly stole my boyfriend.

"My ex," I answer.

"Do you want to leave?" Hudson asks in a lowered voice.

I shake my head. "No, it's fine." I grab another roll. "I'm good."

He doesn't look convinced. "Do you still have feelings for him?"

I hate being asked that question. "God, no. Our relationship wasn't healthy. What bothers me is I'm scared I'll never have that."

"Have what?"

"Someone who looks at me like he does her. Real love. The shit they preach about in the movies they want me to star in." I rub at my eyes.

Don't cry. Please don't cry.

Hudson takes a sip of his water. "Why do you think you'll never have that?"

I shrug. "I don't know."

"You're young, Stella. Give it time. Don't give up."

"You haven't given up on love?"

"Fuck no. I won't let a cheating woman stop me from marrying, having kids, and ending up a happy man. Cameron's betrayal was only a speed bump in my life, and her behavior won't force me to live the rest of my life alone. Fuck that. I'll end up happier than I would've been with her."

I take a deep breath, feeling like it's my turn to share something personal. "My only dating experience is him and a fake boyfriend. I'm not sure I even know what love is. I thought I loved Knox, and it hurt like a bitch when we broke up, but maybe that's because it's all I ever knew. But after a while, it almost felt like a relief. We weren't meant to be, and it was time we quit wasting our time. You know what I'm saying?"

He smiles. "No explanation needed. My dating history is worse than yours. One girlfriend. No fake ones. I'm the wrong person to judge or offer advice on one's love life."

I give him a hard look. "I told you no more talk about fake relationships."

"Are you still in one?" He leans forward, resting his elbows on the table. "It would make me incredibly happy if you weren't."

"I think you know the answer to that."

The awkward silence returns.

His voice is the one to break the tension. "Was your ex also in the business?"

"You really don't know who he is?"

"I wouldn't ask if I did."

"He's Knox Rivers."

His nose wrinkles in disbelief. "You dated that dude?"

"Sure did." I can tell he's heard the stories about Knox. Most of them aren't good. "He wasn't always like that. People change. He was different when we were sixteen. He was monogamous and not the guy who only banged models."

"He cheated on you?"

"No." It's the truth, but people don't believe me. "We broke up and got back together a lot. Sometimes two or three times a week. It was during those times we'd hook up with other people. Never when we were together."

"Sounds like a stable relationship."

"Very stable. I think us going through the phases of stardom together gave us a bond we were afraid of breaking. We understood each other's lives and leaned on each other when people were making ours hell."

"Your parents weren't there for you?"

I shake my head. "That's another reason we clicked. Both of our fathers were absent from our lives … until we made it big, of course. Our moms were also similar: there every step of the way, taking money from us until they could survive on their own *with that money.* I haven't heard from my mom in weeks." I shake my head and release a bitter laugh when it hits me.

"What?"

"You have the picture-perfect family, and I barely have one."

"Every family has its problems. I'd never judge you for something you can't control."

"I wish I had what you do. A happy home." I stare at him, smiling at the thought. Whatever lucky woman who steals Hudson's heart is going to have a great life, and I'm already jealous of her.

"I was blessed with that, yes. Being a good man like my father is one of my biggest goals."

I smile. "That's adorable."

He looks almost offended when he leans in to whisper to me. "Don't refer to me as adorable again, Hollywood. I'm not a pretty boy or any of that shit that you're used to. I don't mind dirt underneath my fingernails. I don't wear tuxedos or do that black-tie bullshit unless it's for a wedding. I'm not adorable. I'm a fucking man."

CHAPTER TWENTY

Stella

I WALK into the living room and collapse on the couch in exhaustion.

It's been a long day.

I glance over at Hudson, sitting in a chair while texting on his phone.

"Alright, smooth talker," I say. "It's time for you to live up to your promise."

He slips the phone into his pocket and gives me his full attention. "Huh?"

"You promised to make up for your asshole behavior earlier. I expect you to honor that."

"How would you like me to do that?"

I smirk. "Preferably naked."

He chuckles, shaking his head. "There are plenty of ways to have fun other than fucking, Hollywood."

"You're right." I hold up my hand and start to count on my fingers as I list off my answers. "There's licking. Sucking. Kissing."

"With no fucking?" he cuts in. "Sounds like all your ideas end up with a bad case of blue balls."

He dodges a pillow when I toss it at him.

"Why do you have to be so complicated?" I groan. "Don't you want to get laid? Hasn't it been like what, a year for you?"

"Only nine months, thank you very much, and there's no disputing I'd enjoy getting laid. You saw my cock earlier, didn't you?"

Damn straight I did.

He was hard as a rock.

I rub my thighs together, remembering how his thick cock had twitched in excitement. "Why are you pulling away then? We want the same thing."

He snaps his fingers. "That's where you're wrong."

"How am I wrong? You playing for the other team now?"

"Pussy is the only field I play in, sweetheart. When I say we don't want the same thing, I'm not referring to sex. I'm in a bad place in my life right now and not sure a no-strings-attached and only fun sex relationship is the best way for me to pull out of it."

I gape at him. "You're in a bad place because of what happened with your ex?"

He drums his fingers against his chin. "She's a part of it, yes, but not all. Cameron cheating isn't the only bad shit that's happened to me."

"You want to talk about it?"

"I don't think a therapy session would be fun for either of us. Shit, it'd probably be a contraceptive more than anything. I'd scare you away."

"Nothing you could say would scare me away."

His gaze darkens. "Trust me on this one."

His face tells me he's finished with this conversation, so I decide to go a different route.

"So, no fucking. No heart-to-heart conversations. What's your plan of making it up to me then? And FYI, I have enough shoes." That's not technically true, but I'm trying to make a point here.

His mood changes from intense to laid-back as a smile builds on his lips. "How about dinner and a board game?"

The fuck?

"Your idea of redemption is feeding me and playing Monopoly? You're such a tease."

He's playing dick games, goddamnit.

"Sure is." He smacks his leg and brings himself up from the chair. "Now, what sounds good for dinner?"

Sex. His cock.

I get up and trail him to the kitchen, pouting the entire way. "How about you surprise me?"

He opens the fridge and starts moving things around. "Let's see what I have to work with." He looks back at me. "I want to give you a heads-up that this won't be my best meal, considering you don't have much in here."

"It will be better than anything I throw together." I stroll over to the wine fridge and grab a bottle before pouring us a glass. I leave his on the counter and take mine as I sit down behind the island. "I'll relax and enjoy the show."

He stops what he's doing to look up at me. "That'll work, but only on one condition."

"What's that?" I have a hateful relationship with conditions. Blame it on Tillie's condition-loving ass.

"You let me pick the game we play."

Is he actually for real about this whole game night thing?

I narrow my eyes at him. "Seriously? I thought you were joking about that."

He shakes his head. "The only way you're getting out of a game is if you put on an apron and start helping."

"Fine, one game."

He grins. "Scrabble it is."

"What's up with you Barnes boys and Scrabble?"

He stops to look up at me again, his brows furrowed. "You played Scrabble with Dallas?" He looks almost pissed off.

"Yes?" I answer, blinking. "The little shit is the most competitive person I know."

"Scrabble is the game of the Barnes family," he explains. "*We're all* competitive. We can't be beat."

I chug down the rest of my glass. "I don't know. I play a pretty mean game."

"Scrabble it definitely is then."

I slide out of my chair to pour myself another glass. "Then a repeat of what happened after yoga?"

He shakes his head. "Seven letters, one word."

"You suck?" I guess. *Not one word, but close enough.*

He laughs. "Nice try."

"Do you not like wine?" I ask, noticing his untouched glass.

He shrugs. "I'm more of a beer guy."

"I'll be sure to have the fridge stocked."

He grins. "Appreciate that."

CHAPTER TWENTY-ONE

Hudson

I'M BUSTING my ass to prepare the perfect meal for Stella.

I know my way around the kitchen, but it's been a while, so I'm a bit rusty. I decide on honey-glazed chicken because I have the recipe down pat. It might sound boring, but it's far from that. My chicken could win awards. It actually did in a Blue Beech cook-off. I'm not claiming to be Bobby Flay, but I can throw down.

My parents made sure we learned from both of them growing up. My dad took us under his wing to work in his repair shop, and my mom spent the weeknights teaching us how to cook and clean. Those cooking lessons paid off when Cameron and I got our own place. My ex's idea of a home-cooked meal was pouring a box of mac and cheese into boiling water. I'd get lucky sometimes, and she'd add hot dogs to her infamous pasta. Her specialty.

But I loved the woman, and when you love someone, you accept their flaws. Over time, you actually start to love them.

Stella sips her wine and keeps her attention on me as I move around the kitchen. I marinate the chicken, slide it in the oven, and start slicing veggies before tossing them in a skillet along with the seasonings. I don't have all the ingredients I need, but there's enough for me to work with.

I'm doing a lousy ass job at keeping our relationship professional already, and I doubt cooking her dinner and drinking together will help that. I consider myself a strong man, but the force of Stella Mendes is breaking me down.

We make conversation, talking to each other in excitement, and words jump from my tongue like fire as we throw out question after question.

We're both giving.

Both taking.

I want to know every detail of her life—every flaw, quirk, every-fucking-thing about her. In order to get that, I give her mine—convincing myself I'll put those bricks back up later. I'll only cave for tonight.

She rolls her eyes and calls me basic when I say my favorite color is green. I laugh when she declares hers is sparkles. Whether it's a real color is decided after a five-minute debate where I'm declared the loser. Her go-to food is tacos and guacamole. I'll remember that for the next time I cook for us. Mine is anything that pairs well with beer. She demands I clarify, and I finally cave in and admit it's burgers and ribs.

She talks me into having a glass of wine. My mouth waters as I load our plates with food. She grabs the bottle of wine, and I carry our plates outside to the patio. One thing I've come to love about Cali is the weather, especially in the evening. It's not too hot. Not too cold.

And the view is incredible.

Stella lights the candles on the table while I set down the plates. I pull out her chair before taking my seat across from her, and then something hits me.

I slide my chair out and get up. "Shit, we forgot glasses."

"Don't worry about it," Stella says, stopping me. She snatches the bottle and takes a drink from it. "It tastes even better this way."

I smirk. "I think I'm rubbing off on you, Hollywood."

"I agree." She leans in with a wild grin on her face. "I like it."

"Oh, really?'

"Yes, really." She looks around the yard. "Thank you for making me dinner and suggesting we eat out here. I've never truly been able to enjoy my backyard like this. I mean, I do yoga occasionally, but other than that, it's never used."

"You're not out here all the time? You couldn't get me to hang out anywhere else if I lived here."

"You do live here."

A smile tugs at my lips. "Good point."

"It's nice enjoying it without the stress. Whenever I entertained, I was always too worried to enjoy it. Everything had to be perfect because I was scared of people judging me. By the time it was all done, it was more of a headache for me."

"Tell me you've at least done something fun out here. Got wild? Skinny-dipped?"

"I wish, but no. I've honestly had such a great time hanging out with you in the kitchen and out here—the places I've never made use of." She picks up her fork but doesn't take a bite. "You make me feel so comfortable and allow me to be *me*. I can drink wine from the bottle and fuck cushions up without you gossiping behind my back."

She snags the cushion from the chair next to her and throws it across the yard.

Why do I feel so excited at her confession?

Why am I lighting up like a fucking firework knowing I make this chick feel good?

And why the fuck am I feeling the same way?

This California air must be fucking with me.

"That's where you're wrong. When you go to bed, I'm calling all my friends and telling them you're a monster for drinking out of the bottle."

She snorts. "I'm so sure."

Our food is getting cold, but I don't care.

I want this conversation.

"This has been an exciting night for me, too," I say.

"Yeah, right." She flips her hair behind her shoulder. "Says the guy who's spent his life protecting people and shooting firearms. You do all kinds of crazy stuff, and Dallas has told me plenty of stories about the trouble you caused when you were younger. I doubt making me dinner and watching me drink is fun for you."

"Not saying it's the best entertainment I've had, but I've never enjoyed getting to know someone as much as I have you, and I've never been so happy about someone proving me wrong."

"Proving you wrong how?"

"About who you are. I was a dickhead for judging you at first."

"At least you have the balls to admit it."

"I'm not afraid to admit I'm not always right." I can write a book of everything I've done wrong in my life, including stopping us on the couch earlier. I should've hunted for a condom.

"Glad I proved you wrong."

Our conversation is interrupted by the sound of her stomach grumbling.

I point at her plate with my fork. "You take the first bite."

"Why?" She narrows her eyes at me. "You trying to poison me?"

I throw my head back. "Jesus, no. It's rude for the chef to take the first bite."

"All right, but FYI, if I'm taking the bite to my death, I stuck a note somewhere in my room that says if I die, you did it."

"Damn, you're untrusting. Taste my food before I take it as an insult."

She cuts off a piece of chicken, takes a bite, and immediately goes in for another. A moan escapes her while she chews, and I shift in my chair. I've never enjoyed watching someone eat.

Maybe it's because she's eating my meat.

Fuck, that was lame.

"Holy hell," she finally says. "This is unbelievable. You weren't kidding about your kitchen skills. Your breakfast was good, but this dinner is incredible. I'll forever be asking you to cook for me. Consider that your new j-o-b."

I hold my hand up. "Whoa there, don't be getting too excited. This won't happen too often."

I go in for my first bite while she takes her third. She wasn't exaggerating to pump up my ego. Even with a few ingredients missing, it's good as fuck.

I'm slower in clearing my plate than she is because I can't stop watching her.

My cooking is good, but it's not the best part of this meal.

It's her. Her company. Her conversation.

I'll never forget my time with Stella. The memories will stay with me as I board a flight to Iowa when it's time to leave and live my life—remembering this as one of my favorite pit stops.

I'll never forget her sipping wine so dark it stains her lips the perfect crimson red, or the view of her taking long breaths between her laughs when she's excited. No matter what, I'll forever remember my time in California with the woman who was out of my league.

I'll always have that *what-if* in the back of my mind.

What if we weren't living in two different worlds?

What if I was willing to give up everything and move here?

What if she was willing to do the same?

"I HAVE A CONFESSION TO MAKE."

I take my last bite and look up at Stella. "Go on."

She sips on her wine, looking guilty. "I'm not exactly a Scrabble master."

I set my napkin down next to me and slide my chair out from under the table. "That's my cue to go. I can't hang out with Scrabble imposters." I gesture to the wine in her hand. "I'm okay with you chugging from that bottle, but lying about Scrabble is where I draw the line."

She rolls her eyes. "The first time I played was with your brother."

"Did you not have a childhood?"

"If by childhood, you mean my mom dragging me from audition to audition and then forcing me to get my hair lightened, then yes, I had the perfect childhood."

My stomach drops at her answer. "Shit, I'm sorry." Her response pisses me off. My parents made us work around the house and do chores, but they never stopped us from going out and having fun.

"It's fine. I eventually had my fun when I started making my own money."

"I take it Scrabble wasn't at the top of that bucket list?"

"Can't say it was. I tried getting Willow to play it with me once, but that girl is the queen of short attention span. We lasted two rounds before she decided we needed to catch up on *Teen Mom*."

"Priorities."

"You know it. Therefore, game night never became a thing for me."

"Surely, you have friends other than her?"

She used to hang out in the clubs with people all the time, at least that's what Lucy told me when Dallas first took the job. She was nervous he'd fall under the seduction of the women around him.

"As of lately, no. I lost most of them in my breakup with Knox."

"What? Like a prenup? You got the curtains and fine china, and he got the crew upon going your separate ways?"

"Something like that. They had to choose, and they chose him." She shrugs. "I'd rather keep to myself now anyway. The last thing I need is someone finding out about this whole Eli scheme and blabbing about it." She's acting like it's nothing, but there's no doubt it bothers her to lose people she thought had her back. Maybe money and fame don't buy happiness.

She scrubs her hands over her face and takes another sip of wine. "I have an idea."

I arch a brow. "Your ideas are never good."

"Let's make a wager."

"Do proceed."

"Scrabble winner gets to choose how we end the night."

"In other words, the winner gets to decide if I spend the entire night fucking you in that pool or not?"

She flinches, my answer catching her off guard, and warmth swims over her cheeks. "Exactly."

"That doesn't make me want to win."

She winks. "Be a gentleman and lose."

"I wouldn't count on it. I told you us Barnes men are competitive about our board games."

"Bring it."

"AROUSAL?" Stella screeches around a fit of laughter so loud I'm sure she woke the neighbors.

We're still outside finishing off our second bottle of wine and battling over Scrabble.

"How the hell did you get those letters?" She reaches over the table, grabs the box, and starts searching through it for evidence I'm cheating. "That can't happen in real life."

I hold up my hands. "Playing fair and square over here,

Hollywood. Don't be pissed because the Scrabble gods are in my favor."

"The Scrabble gods must be trying to tell you something if you have the letters to spell arousal."

She has a point.

My mind is still blown that I'm trying to win when the outcome of losing means we have sex.

I point at the board. "Your turn."

She runs her manicured hand over her chin and dramatically debates her next move. Her eyes squint before a sly smile spreads across her plump lips. I run a finger over my mouth and remember how delicious she tasted this morning.

I scoot forward while watching her spell out her word, and my mouth drops when she finishes.

"Balls deep?" I question, going back over the letters as if there's a mistake.

And she thinks my ass is cheating?

"That's two words."

"Says who, Webster?"

I signal down to my lap. "Says the guy with balls."

She rolls her eyes. "Okay, well says the girl who's had her fair share of working with balls, I get some say." Her hand flies to her lips as her face turns red. "Dear God, can we act like those words never left my mouth? This is what happens when I drink too much wine. I start talking about my experience with balls." She smacks her forehead. "See! There I go again!"

I can't help but burst out in laughter, and she gives me a look that falls between dirty and annoyance.

She's right about the alcohol. It's getting to us. I never imagined I'd play Scrabble so damn kinky. Add Stella and booze to the equation, and this is the best damn game night I've ever had.

"Care to share some of those working experiences?" I ask but then stop her before she answers. "Scratch that. I don't want to hear about any of your past experiences. I'd rather you show me about how you work with them and let me experience it myself." I glance down at my now-stirring cock growing more excited from this *balls talk*.

She jumps up from her chair. "Excuse me while I go drown myself."

I stand, meeting her at the pool, and spin her around to face me. "Come on, it'll look bad on my resume if my employer drowns while I'm on the job. Don't be embarrassed. My dick likes your balls talk."

She attempts to pull away to block her face, but I stop her. "I appreciate you trying to make me feel better and all, but that so did not turn you on."

I move my hand to hers and bring it straight to my aching erection. She doesn't flinch or move her hand.

This action right here seals our fate.

"Still think I'm lying?"

She massages me. "Possibly, but all the evidence hasn't been seen. Remove the pants."

"Let me convince you with Exhibit B then."

Her eyes widen and follow my every move when I take a step back. Nervousness drives through me like a bullet when I unbuckle my jeans. Anticipation rises at the sound of my zipper going down. Any thoughts I've had about not touching Stella again are long gone.

Nothing will cure this sexual tension but sex.

I've been jacking off for days in an attempt to get over my attraction to her, but it hasn't helped. I'm harder than I've ever been, and I haven't even touched her yet.

She gasps when I drop my pants and boxer briefs, and I stand in front of her in all my naked glory. The backyard is secluded, and I'm hoping none of her stalkers are creeping around and get a shot of my dick … or one of Stella when I pound into her pussy soon.

She stays quiet, her eyes glued to me, and I glance down at my pulsating cock.

The fuck?

It's hard as a rock—not flaccid or any other weird shit, so what's going on? She's been up-front about wanting my dick, but now that I'm handing it to her, she's mute?

Maybe she's rethinking this.

Maybe her plan was to get me all worked up and then walk away like I did her.

I'd deserve it.

I clear my throat. "A little quiet over there."

"Just taking in the view," she says.

"And?"

"Not bad."

"Just not bad?"

She chews on the tip of her nail. "I mean you know what they say about cars. It can look nice, but what really matters is the acceleration and speed behind it. What's under the hood. What do you have for Exhibit C?"

"How about I show you?"

From the shit-eating grin on her face, it's clear she wants my dick, but there's something more mischievous on her agenda. I lift my shirt over my head and throw it down before getting closer.

I thank the good man above that I have kick-ass reflexes, in large part to Dallas picking on my ass for years until I learned how to defend myself, because as soon as she goes to push me in the pool, I grab her arm, taking her with me. Holding in a breath, we go under and gasp for air while resurfacing.

"I show you my dazzling cock, and that's what I get in return?" I ask, catching my breath and shaking my head. "So ungrateful."

She's laughing. "You didn't have to throw me in with you."

"Oh, yes, I did."

Because we're about to have some fun.

CHAPTER TWENTY-TWO

Stella

MY BREATHING DRAGS, my lungs working on overdrive, while we stare at each other underneath the bright moonlight.

Hudson's perfect, hard, his hard cock making my mouth water. His hand is cold when he reaches out to capture my waist, and he pulls me into his muscular chest. Our eyes meet when he stares down at me with a sin-filled grin. I moan when our eye contact breaks, and his erection brushes my thigh.

I'm terrified but eager for his next move.

Our lips are only inches apart.

"Looks like you won, Hollywood."

He's so damn close I can feel his heart beating against mine.

I tilt my head to the side, licking my lips. "What do you mean?"

"The wager. You won. Tell me what the loser needs to do to redeem himself."

I don't give him an answer.

Well, *I do* … but not with words.

It's with my lips crashing into his with urgency and desperation.

He groans into my mouth, slipping his tongue through, and guides us to the shallow end of the pool, our connection never parting. I moan when I'm pushed against the wall, and his strong arms cage me in, one going to each side of my body.

His tongue plunges farther into my mouth, skillfully massaging it against mine.

This kiss is aggressive. Abrasive. We're devouring an act denied for too long. He pulls at the hem of my top before ripping it right down the middle.

Yes, he fucking rips it.

And throws it on the ground like it is last season's Gucci.

I break away to give him a dirty look. "That's my favorite shirt." It was also expensive as fuck.

"*Was* your favorite shirt," he corrects. "It looked expensive, and I didn't want it to suffer more water damage. I heard that's bad for fine silk. Which is why this is the next to go."

He unsnaps my bra and tosses it next to my shirt. I'm about to praise him for caring about my precious lingerie, but all words stop when he traces my nipples with his tongue before latching onto it, sucking hard.

I'm screaming at myself when I push at his shoulders to stop him. "No condom again," I whisper, my voice trembling. My vagina and brain are having a showdown. One wants to stop this before it ends terribly. The other doesn't care as long as he keeps doing that thing with his tongue. "If that's still your rule, stop now. Don't lead me on and do that shit again, or I might take my dinner knife and castrate you."

My threat might be a little overdramatic, but whatever.

Getting someone worked up and then walking away is quite possibly the most overdramatic thing you can do, right?

"You need to make a decision." It's not a request. It's a command.

"I won't stop," he softly assures me. "If that's okay with you?"

He moves in closer while waiting for my answer.

"I'm clean, and I trust you are," he goes on. Water flies from his hair when he shakes his head. "What I said earlier came out wrong. I have shitty delivery, and I'm sorry."

He puts some distance between us and tilts his head forward to run his tongue between my breasts.

Hell yes.

How the fuck is everything he does so damn hot?

He pushes into my touch when I reach down and start stroking his shaft. I love the sound of him moaning in my ear while he slides his hands down my sides and hitches my legs around his hips, giving me a better sense of how hard he is for me.

Another gasp leaves me at the temperature change when he walks us up the pool steps and straight to the outdoor furniture area. My heart is hammering so hard I can feel it against my throat when he carefully lays me down on the couch and takes a step back.

He licks his lips, drinking in the sight of my half-naked body on display for him.

I hold in a breath when he leans down and unsnaps my shorts, dragging them down my legs and tossing them to the side. A burst of energy rushes through me when he drops to his knees at my side and teasingly rubs me through my panties.

I arch my back, begging for more, and loving the stimulation of the lace caressing my clit.

He's not even directly touching me where I want him yet has me on the top of the orgasm ladder. He doesn't let up until I'm almost to my brink, *almost right fucking there.*

That's when he pulls away. It wouldn't be a moment with Hudson if he didn't start fucking with my mind and orgasm in some way.

"What the hell?" I scream. "I told you to let me know if you were going to change your mind!"

I narrow my eyes but take the time to admire the view of his cock close-up. The tip glistens with pre-come, and I almost fall off the couch when he slowly strokes it once.

That's my job.

What I'm supposed to be doing.

"Hollywood, there's no way I'm walking away from you tonight. I'm only getting started."

"Then get started! Why are you still standing there?"

I'm not a virgin, nor am I worried about him making it romantic. All I need is an orgasm, and this girl is good to go. That's probably why I've had such a great relationship with handheld electronics lately.

He glances from side to side. "You sure you're okay with us doing it here?"

I can't help but laugh at how ridiculous we probably look. He's standing in front of me with a massive boner while giving me a damn questionnaire. Meanwhile, I'm spread out on my pool furniture wearing only panties.

"Yes. Now, fuck me," I demand.

He grins and strokes his cock one last time before moving to the end of the couch. My panties are off in a flash—flying through the air at the same time he slides up my body and hovers over me.

We do one of our infamous stare downs.

The horniest stare down in history.

Our lips meet again, igniting a passion stronger than anything I've ever experienced. I break away, my lips roaming down his neck to his hard nipple, and I tug at it with my teeth.

It's hypnotic the way we move together so effortlessly. His fingers and tongue seem to know all my sensitive spots.

I'm sweaty, and my heart is racing by the time he sweeps my hair back, meets my gaze, and slowly pushes inside me. I tilt my hips up to take every inch of him while adjusting to his large size.

I've never had sex with anyone without a condom before. Knox and I never had sex without protection. Besides being terrified of having children, our managers provided us with every birth control method known to man.

Hudson doesn't break eye contact when he withdraws and slams back inside me. My breasts bounce while he pumps into me, and his hands travel up to squeeze them. I spread my legs wider, and his balls smack against my ass. His tongue is cold when he sucks on my nipple, and I nearly lose it when his mouth returns to mine. He slows his pace, which isn't how I want it tonight.

I need rough and hard.

Like earlier, he thinks he's running the show.

One thing I need to teach Hudson Barnes is that I like being in charge, too.

"I want to be on top," I moan, writhing underneath him.

I gasp when he pulls out, helps me up, and then falls down on the couch in a sitting position, his legs spread apart.

He grins while I nervously stand in front of him and starts stroking himself. I inhale a breath and straddle him, shuddering as I sink down on his erection. He drops his head forward to stare at our connection. I run my fingers through his wet hair and pull at the roots while slowly starting to ride him.

"Fuck yes," he moans. "Ride me just like that."

I've taken the control from Hudson—a man who likes to have it at all times. But he doesn't seem to care as I take every inch of him.

He's abandoning his dominance.

I'm abandoning my gracefulness.

"Does that dick feel good, Hollywood?" he hisses through clenched teeth.

"Yes, so damn good," I groan around other words that I'll blush tomorrow.

I'm trembling, my legs tangled and shaking against his, but nothing is holding me back.

It's as if I'm on top of the world.

Well, on top of the world's best cock.

He palms my ass and rocks his hips up, our movements at the perfect pace until we're both moaning and sweating. I bite into my lip when my orgasm hits before collapsing against him. Hudson shudders while coming inside me and rests his head on my shoulder as we catch our breath. My stomach knots as I avert my gaze, sweeping over the yard, and I hesitate before looking down at him.

I'm nervous.

Terrified.

Did we get caught up in the moment?

Does he regret this?

His hand glides up my back, and he strokes my skin while smiling up at me.

I can't help but laugh at myself for being so worried. Hudson isn't that kind of guy. He won't give me a pat on the back and then walk away.

"I think I won the game tonight," I whisper. My pitch embarrassingly rises like I have a sore throat. That's most likely not the only part of my body that's in for a sore morning.

He brushes my hair away from my sweaty face. "No, Hollywood. You riding my dick like that made me win at life."

CHAPTER TWENTY-THREE

Stella

I HAVE A NEW FAVORITE.

Shower sex.

More specifically, shower sex with Hudson.

That's how I started my wonderful morning.

We stayed in the shower until the water turned cold, and Hudson helped me dry off. He went to his room to change and have his daily checkup call with his family. I love how close he is with them.

I grab my phone from my nightstand and collapse on my bed, my feet hanging over the edge, and notice a missed call from Willow.

My phone rang earlier, but I was on my knees with Hudson's cock in my mouth, so unfortunately, she got sent to voicemail. I love my friend and all … but sex.

Again, *shower sex.*

Wet bodies.

Wet everything.

I can't stop grinning when I hit her name.

"It's about time you called my ass back," she says. "I've been calling you for hours."

"It's been *twenty minutes,*" I correct. "Calm your tits."

She laughs. “My tits are very calm over here … and very much neglected as well. It sucks being single.”

“You know what that calls for,” I sing out.

“Benny, my lovely vibrator, who never seems to let me down. By the way, that was the worst birthday present. I told you I wanted a unicorn. Not an orgasm generated with double A’s.”

“You’ll be thanking me for it as you venture into singlehood. Trust me, nothing cures the heart of a bad breakup like some good self-induced orgasms.”

“Eh, you’re probably right. Now, on to more important things. How bad do you miss me?” She’s taking this breakup better than I thought she would. That … or she’s putting up a front.

“You’ve been gone?”

“Funny. Are you almost dead over there? Are you feeding yourself? Bathing? Taking your multi-vitamin?”

“You do know I’m twenty-five, not three, right? Although I do miss your help.”

“Anything new? How did your audition go? I haven’t heard anything back, but I know Susie said agents have been calling about you because of the hype from *Forever Ago*.”

Susie is my manager, who mostly communicates through Willow unless she has a new part or a possible deal she wants me to look at.

“The script was an absolute nightmare. Fingers crossed I don’t get the part.”

“There’s my optimistic best friend. I didn’t get a chance to read it. That bad, huh?”

“Yep.” I study my fingernails and blow out a long breath. “I hooked up with Hudson.” My mouth blurts out the words. The need to tell *someone* has been killing me.

Is this a bad idea?

Am I stupid?

I need some advice here.

I’ve never had a no-strings attached relationship, so I’m not sure how to go about doing this.

Am I allowed to tell Willow?

Is he going to tell Dallas?

A moment of silence passes.

"What do you mean hooked up?" she finally asks.

"You know ... *hooked up.*"

What the hell?

Saying you hooked up is like saying peanut butter goes with jelly.

Do I need to whip out dolls and show her what parts went where?

"What's your definition of hooked up? Like you guys made out for a minute or did anal?"

"Oh my god, Willow!" I yell, nearly rolling off my bed as she breaks out into a fit of laughter.

"You have to be more specific, girl. I never know with you."

"You never know with me? I'm not the anal sex queen. Jesus!"

"Now, give me all the details."

"Well, the first time—"

"Hold up, girlfriend," she interrupts. "There's been more than one time, and you're just now telling me this? What the hell?"

"I didn't know I needed to report to you when I get laid."

"You do when it's with your hot bodyguard—who you've sworn you're staying away from. I need *every detail.*"

"You're going through a breakup. I don't want to be insensitive."

"That's not insensitive. It actually makes me feel better hearing my best friend is getting some good dick. Just because I'm down doesn't mean I want everyone around me to be down and sex-deprived."

This is why Willow is my best friend. She'll ask about your day when hers was hell, and cheer for you from the sidelines when you're falling in love, even when she's going through a breakup.

I make myself comfortable and tell her everything. I've had more orgasms in the past few days than I've had in months. Hudson might not have been intimate with a list full of women, but he definitely has plenty of experience.

"What are you going to do now?" she asks when I finish. "Date him? Is it casual? I mean, won't it be complicated with the Eli situation?" Willow begged me not to agree to the Eli deal, but I didn't listen to her.

I play with my hair, twirling strands around my finger. "I don't know. I like him and enjoy spending time with him. He gets me."

"Are there feelings?"

"Yes, and that scares me."

"Why?"

"He's going back to Iowa as soon as we hire someone else. What happens then? Will we shake hands, say thanks for the sex, and never speak again? I insisted it'd be a no-strings-attached fling, but he's told me plenty of times he's never been into an arrangement like that."

"Long-distance relationships can work. My situation isn't the best example, but you and Knox were good for a while."

There's optimism but also concern in her voice. In this industry, so many long-distance relationships have fallen apart.

Shoot, it's not even just in this industry.

Distance ruined Hudson and his fiancé's relationship. They say the heart doesn't notice miles, but I call bullshit. It notices when you're going to bed alone, the insecurities, and the panic that pumps through you when you haven't heard from them for hours.

Are they hurt?

With someone else?

Distance is hard on the heart.

"Knox and I were good at faking," I say—the excitement of my morning fading.

"Don't pull away while he's there. Give it a chance. If things don't work out, look on the bright side. You won't have to worry about running into him again."

"Good point." I've been dodging anywhere Knox hangs out, and if Hudson weren't with me yesterday, I would've stormed out of the restaurant the moment they walked in.

"Promise you'll give it a chance. Do it for me and my broken heart."

"*Fine*, I'll do it for you."

She snorts. "I know you love me and all, but you're doing this more for yourself and your vagina."

"*Onto* the next subject. How are you doing?"

"I haven't been back to the hospital and moved my shit back to my mom's. My biggest issue is Brett's bitch sisters. They're pissed I burned his sneakers before leaving. I took pictures and sent them to his phone, so he'd know they were gone. It'd be rude for him to stress finding the perfect shoes for his next date."

I chuckle, shaking my head. "How did I know you'd do something to make him pay? You're having too much fun with this."

"Burning shit mends a broken heart. The flames bring out a whole new you. I'm ready to find myself, change my hair, do all that *new me* crap they talk about in self-help books. My mom's been sending me Pinterest quotes about moving on."

"Is it working?"

"The Pinterest quotes? Hell no. I don't want to be that sad girl who looks on the bright side. I want to be the bitch who goes on a revenge spree. Burning his shit, writing he's a cheater on his car, maybe hunt down one of his friends and sleep with him … or all of them."

I laugh. She's so lying. Willow has only been with Brett, and I don't see her going on a one-night stand binge.

"You do know he's in the hospital right now? Don't you feel kind of bad for him?"

"Yes, which is the only reason I haven't kicked his balls into his stomach."

CHAPTER TWENTY-FOUR

Hudson

I HAVEN'T SPENT much time with Stella today.

It fucking sucks.

I went from dreading the days with her to looking forward to them.

Now that I've had a taste of her, I can't get enough. If I woke up every morning with the taste of her on my tongue, I'd be one happy motherfucker.

We slept in our own beds last night. I could see she wanted me to stay with her, but I'm not ready for that yet. I can't scare her off. When she asked to join her in the shower this morning, there was no saying no.

Her schedule has been jam-packed, and people have been in and out of the house all day. She made conference calls with her agent, and her stylist came over with a shit ton of clothing. My free time has been spent hanging out in my room and searching for new job prospects.

My father took over my grandfather's business after he passed and wants me to work for him. I grew up in the repair shop that specializes in engines and large farming equipment and has been in my family for over sixty years. Like Grandfather did, our dad expects Dallas or me to take over when he retires.

That'd been my plan after promising Cameron I wouldn't deploy again. I've worked on equipment ten times my size since I was fifteen, and I'd enjoy it. But first, I have to get my shit together. My dad made it clear he wasn't handing the company over to anyone not settled.

Growing up, we were given a checklist in life. Find a wife, have children, and work hard until retirement. Live life to the fullest. Be happy. My mom would say this every night before bed without fail. Having fun is cool but only after our responsibilities are met.

My phone beeps at the same time I shut my laptop after sending my final email.

Stella: I'm having a pizza delivered in 5 minutes. Will you answer the door and bring it up to me in the gym?

Me: Only if you share.

Stella: Duh.

My stomach growls at the thought of pizza. The majority of Stella's food is health-nut bullshit. Gluten-free this. No high-fructose syrup that. I've forgotten what real sugar tastes like.

When the alert goes off that someone is approaching the gate, I glance at the video screen in the corner of my bedroom. I buzz the delivery guy through, and the delicious scent of greasy cheese hits me when I open the door. My stomach growls when I tip him, and I grab plates and drinks from the kitchen before going upstairs.

"Pizza delivery," I call out, walking into the gym.

Stella smiles and hops off the treadmill without bothering to turn it off. I size her up as she struts toward me in a sports bra and workout pants. Her hair is in a loose ponytail, and sweat trickles down her chest and between her breasts. I lick my lips, craving her more than the pizza.

"Finally," she moans. "I'm starving."

Her moan matches the one she makes when we're having

sex. I guess my sex game is on the same excitement scale as pizza.

She opens the box while it's in my hands and pulls out a slice. After taking a bite, she moves back to the treadmill, the slice still in her hand, and goes back to working out.

I set the pizza box on a weight bench. "What are you doing?"

Her forehead creases together while she looks over at me, keeping her pace. "Eating dinner?" She plucks off a pepperoni and pops it in her mouth.

"On the treadmill?"

She nods.

"You're eating pizza on the treadmill?"

This woman is a nutjob.

"Sure am." She points at the box. "You better get yourself a slice before I eat it all."

I keep staring at her.

"Are you not hungry?"

"My mind is too busy trying to figure out why you're eating pizza on the treadmill."

"Haven't you ever heard of multitasking? My agent was up my ass *about my ass* today. I looked heavy in a few bikini pictures that were leaked, so I need to tone this up." She smacks her ass. "My problem is that my soul mate is carbs. Therefore, in order for me to give in to my one true love, I have to work out."

The fuck?

"Sweetheart, you are not fat and are being too hard on yourself. And fuck your agent for making you feel less than perfect." I scrub my hand over my jaw and level my eyes on her. "That ass is perfection. Your hips, fucking flawless, especially when I grip them while you're riding my cock."

Hollywood is a bunch of sugar-hating, green smoothie-drinking dickheads.

She almost loses her step at my response but manages to correct herself. "Thank you. I'm glad you appreciate this ass. I only wish your opinion was the same as everyone else in the business."

"Someone else's opinion of your body shouldn't define how you feel about yourself. You're beautiful."

Bitterness fills my mouth, and I wonder how many people have tried to change her. From her mom forcing her to color her hair to the people who work for her complaining about her weight.

She flashes me a shy smile and holds up the last bite of pizza before popping it in her mouth. "If I want to eat like this, I have to work it off."

I beckon her with my finger. "Come here."

She shakes out her arms while staring at me skeptically. I stand quietly until she does what I asked. She jumps off the treadmill, and I plant my hands on her hips. She gasps when I turn her around in my arms and guide us to the mirrored wall. We stare at our reflection as I hold her in place.

"You know what I see?" I whisper into her ear.

She shivers but stays quiet.

"A beautiful woman—inside and out. Don't fucking listen to anyone who tells you otherwise."

Her eyes meet mine, and her plump lips curl into a smile. "Who would've thought underneath that tough exterior was a man so comforting? There's a spot of understanding in you that I've never found with anyone else. No matter what happens to my career, my money, or my appearance, I have a feeling it'll never change the way you look at me."

I gulp. "Never."

She shifts in my hold, turning to face me, and clasps her hands around my neck. When her lips meet mine, I kiss her softly.

"I think you were sent to California for a bigger reason than to be my security guard."

"You're right." I kiss her again. "That reason was you."

A connection this strong doesn't just happen. We were

pushed together to prove we're capable of love, receiving and giving it, and to show us there's a light at the end of the tunnel of our broken hearts. We're two heartbroken souls looking out for one another.

My breathing hitches when she releases me to fall to her knees at the same time as my shorts are pulled down. My cock is already hard at the sight of her innocently staring up at me while biting her lip, and it springs forward in front of her.

I wrap her ponytail around my hand, and her locks spill forward when I undo it from the band. I rake my fingers through her soft strands when she wraps those beautiful lips around the tip of my cock, sucking hard. There's no taking my eyes off her while she slowly draws me into her mouth. I tighten my grip on her hair and guide her just how I like it, even though it doesn't seem she needs my help. I hardly blink while I take in the breathtaking sight in front of me. Her head bobs on my cock, and the sensation of her moans vibrating against my shaft is killing me.

My muscles tense, and before I come, I warn her in case she wants to pull away. She doesn't. I release her hair and stroke her cheek as she swallows my come.

"How do I taste?" I ask.

She runs her tongue along her bottom lip. "Better than any pizza or dessert in the world."

I'm light-headed while coming down from the high of my cock being in Stella's sweet mouth. I help her up to her feet and guide her straight to a seated weight bench. A gasp leaves her when I retreat a step and pull down her pants and panties to her ankles—not bothering to have her kick them off. My cock is hard again when I twist her around and bend her over, her ass in the air. Her back arches at the same time I slide inside her.

She rests her palms on the front of the seat and throws her head back to look at me. "I have a feeling I'm about to work that pizza off."

"I'VE DEFINITELY WORKED up an appetite now," Stella says.

We're sitting on the floor, panting, and trying to catch our breath after the best workout of my life. Hands fucking down, I'll never see a view as hot as Stella bent over a weight bench taking my cock.

I drag the pizza box to us. "You deserve this, babe. No doubt you burned every calorie you've eaten this month from fucking me so hard."

She grabs a slice and takes it with both hands. "I'm almost too exhausted to feed myself."

I set my piece on the floor and grab hers—positioning it at her mouth while she opens and takes a bite.

She laughs after swallowing it. "We're sitting on the floor, sans pants, and stuffing our faces with pizza."

"I have a feeling this is the most romantic post-sex situation there's ever been."

We spend the next five minutes finishing our food and chugging water. I'm chewing my last bite when Stella's mood shift into something that resembles nervousness.

"Tell me what's on your mind," I tell her.

She waves off my question. "It's nothing."

"Tell me what's on your mind."

She crosses her legs, and her nervousness morphs into shyness. "Will you sleep in my bed tonight?"

I grin. "Are you ready to take this relationship to the next level, Hollywood?"

She pushes my shoulder. "I'm serious."

"I'd love nothing more than to share your bed with you."

She looks up at me with a smile.

"Only because I'm sure it's a lot more comfortable than mine."

She rolls her eyes. "You're so damn annoying." She pauses.

"I mean … is that taking a step too far in a *casual sexual relationship*? This is all new to me."

"You do remember I've only fucked one other chick in my life? It's new to us both. How about this: we make our own rules since neither one of us knows what's in the sex only relationship playbook? Sound good?"

She nods. "Sounds good."

CHAPTER TWENTY-FIVE

Stella

I HAVEN'T BEEN this happy in so long.

My bed has never felt so comfortable as it does when I'm wrapped in Hudson's arms. His legs are tangled in mine, and the heat of his chest is perfection against my back.

All night, I've been swept into a cheesy-happy phase. I'm scared to shut my eyes and sleep.

What if I wake up and it's not real?

Now that Hudson is opening up to me, I'm terrified to lose him.

I was on an orgasm high when I invited him into my bed, and surprisingly, the casual sex talk didn't have me running for the hills. It cleared up so much of my confusion … but not *all* of it. What's in his head is a mystery.

Are his feelings as deep as mine?

He's letting me in—something he hasn't done with many people and is hard for him. That tells me I'm edging myself inside him.

Will he allow me to stay?

Or am I only a pit stop in his journey?

My head aches at the thought of him leaving me and falling for a woman from *his world.* A woman his mom loves and who enjoys similar things. A woman who'll build a life with him in his hometown.

Me?

I've discovered I don't need a man who blends in with my lifestyle anymore.

It hasn't worked out well for me in the past.

All I care about is being happy.

Finally, I've found a good man, and I don't know how long he's staying.

I'm startled when his lips go to my ear, and he whispers, "Everything okay? I'm not squeezing the life out of you, am I?"

I shake my head as goose bumps crawl up my arms. "No … just having trouble sleeping. You're still awake?"

"There's something I need to tell you." Nervousness is laced along his words. "I'm only telling you this *in case* it happens. The last thing I want to do is scare the shit out of you … or for you to think there's something wrong with me."

I gulp. "Go on."

"It's embarrassing."

"What? Do you piss the bed or something?"

He chuckles. "I wish it were as easy as controlling my bladder. I have dreams."

"I think almost everyone does."

"Let me rephrase it for you. They're more along the lines of nightmares … flashbacks … of shit that I've witnessed but never want to think about again."

I shift in his arms.

I need to face him for this.

He can't see my face, but I want him to know I'm here for him.

No matter what, dreams or no dreams, I'll never ask him to leave my bed.

"Like PTSD?" I ask.

"Yes. It's the worst the first few weeks I'm home, but over

time, they decline. It took six months to get rid of them last time."

His confession sends a bolt of pain through me. I can't imagine being afraid to fall asleep … scared of what will haunt you when your eyes close.

"Have you had any since you've been home this time? Since you've been here?"

"Every night."

There's a moment of silence.

"Cameron would wake me up and tell me to stop. According to her, I tossed and turned and made weird sounds. I wanted to give you a heads-up, just in case."

I rub his shoulder. "You'd never scare me. You make me feel safer than anyone." I grab his hand. "Do you want to talk about it?"

"I don't want to burden you."

"You can tell me. I want to know anything you're willing to give. I'm all ears, Hudson. I'm all yours."

Give me anything.

Give me it all.

Open your heart.

Open your wounds.

Let me try to heal them.

Those words are on the tip of my tongue, but the fear of him leaving my bed stops me from releasing them.

"I've seen stuff I wish I didn't. I've eaten breakfast with men, they've shown me pictures of their families, their pregnant wives, babies, and then saw them die hours later. I've dragged children …" His voice cracks, and his pain bleeds through the room. "I've dragged children out of rubble … some of them … dead. Some alive. Their faces … they haunt me." He kisses my forehead. "Maybe with you in my arms, I'll sleep better."

I sigh dramatically. "I guess I'll have to do it then."

He chuckles in my ear. "You're amazing. Thank you."

I smile.

CHAPTER TWENTY-SIX

Hudson

THE SHRILL of my phone ringing wakes me, and the sheets moving tells me it did the same with Stella.

It's early, nowhere near sunrise, and I release her to scoot to the edge of her bed. I grab my phone, and fear rips through me when I see Dallas's name on the screen.

This isn't a call to chat.

It's a call that's going to wreck my world.

I hurriedly answer, shoving the phone to my ear, and my heart pounds against my chest so hard I can feel it in my ears. "What happened?"

"It's Lucy." His voice breaks. If he goes on, he's going to lose it.

"I'm on my way."

"Thank you, brother."

The call ends.

I roll out of bed and start to shuffle around the room as quietly as I can, hoping Stella can fall back asleep. I snag my pants and attempt to shove my foot through the leg, but it's difficult to do.

Maybe it's the nerves.

I freeze when the light turns on. Stella yawns as she pulls her hand away from the lamp and situates herself with her back against the headboard.

"Hudson," she whispers.

"Yeah?"

"You're trying to put my pants on."

I look down and realize I'm trying to squeeze into white skinny jeans. I pull them off my foot and lay them over a chair.

"What's going on?" she asks in concern.

"That was Dallas."

We exchange nervous looks. She knows but isn't going to insinuate anything.

"What did he say?"

"Lucy is gone." My voice sounds almost lifeless.

Her hand flies up to her mouth. Even though she suspected it, it's still a shock. "Oh my God. I'm so sorry."

I run a hand through my hair. "I hate to do this since Willow is gone, but I have to find someone to cover for me. I'm sorry, Stella, but I need to go home."

She nods. "I understand. There's no way I'd let you stay."

"Do you have any idea how fast we can get a replacement? Is there an agency or something we can go through?" I grab my pants when I spot them on the other side of the room and have no trouble getting dressed this time.

"There's no need for that. I'm coming with you."

I stop mid-zip of my fly. "I'm sorry, what?"

"I'm coming with you to Iowa."

I'm staring at her, my mouth gaping.

"Dallas is my friend. I want to be there for both of you." She shyly looks down and studies her hands. "I mean … if that's okay with you."

"I'm always okay with having you around, but are you sure it's a good idea? Won't Tillie have your ass?"

"I don't give a shit what she thinks is a good idea at the moment. I'll get my bags packed and ask Willow to book us a flight."

"Thank you for this." It's a big step for her … for us. She's coming to Blue Beech as a support system for me … for my family.

"You don't have to thank me for being there for you, Hudson. You've been doing it for me since the moment you walked into my home."

CHAPTER TWENTY-SEVEN

Stella

WILLOW BOOKED us the first private flight she could, and I threw everything I needed in my suitcase before rushing to the airport with Hudson.

Our flight won't take us straight to Blue Beech since it's in the middle of bum-fuck-Egypt, so we'll take a car the rest of the way.

"Willow wanted me to tell you that she's sorry for your loss," I say after the pilot informs us that he's ready for takeoff.

Devastation has taken over Hudson. It's everywhere—on his face, the way he moves, how he's barely spoken ten words since we left the house. And those words were only telling me how grateful he was that I'm doing this for him.

He gives me an artificial smile. "Tell her thank you."

Dallas told me stories about Lucy. They started dating in the days of recess, and his family saw her as their family.

"Have you ever been to Iowa?" he asks.

My stomach settles at his push for conversation. I've never lost anyone close to me, so I can't connect with him in that way. The only loss I've ever dealt with is a relationship, and that's not shit compared to death.

"No," I answer. "But Dallas has described it pretty well. He said it's one of those small towns where people are in their own little world. Ones people think only exists on TV shows. You borrow sugar and milk from each other and leave your doors unlocked."

I shudder. That shit would never happen in LA.

Robbers. Rapists. Fucking psychopaths.

It'd be a cold day in hell before I left my bedroom unlocked, let alone my front door.

"That's Blue Beech," he says with a hint of a smile. "Living in a small town has its ups and downs, but I wouldn't trade it for anything. There's always something that feels good about going home."

"You would never move away or live anywhere else?" I ask the question casually but am dying to hear his answer.

He shakes his head. "All I need in life is family and a good place to come home to. That's Blue Beech for me."

His answer is sweet, but that doesn't stop it from plunging pain through me. My naïve dream that Hudson would pack up and move into my house is nothing but that—a dream. He'll never be mine because I can't be that girl for him. There aren't career opportunities in Blue Beech.

The career or the man.

Which one would be harder to lose?

My phone beeps with a text.

"Willow wants to know where to book my room," I read out loud.

I want to stay with Hudson but can't assume that's an option.

"This will make me sound like a bum, but my ex kept the place we were renting. I haven't had a chance to look for anything else. You have three options: We can crash at Dallas's or my parents' house, you can stay at the bed and breakfast in town, or there's a hotel an hour away from town, but trust me, it's not anywhere you'd want to stay."

That's somewhat of an invite to stay with him, right?

Unfortunately, he laid the decision at my feet. Inviting myself into someone else's home feels uncomfortable, especially since I've already invited myself to Iowa in the first place.

"I can stay at the bed and breakfast. I'll have Willow book it for me. Do you know the name of it?"

He cups his hand over my knee and squeezes it. "I do, but I was hoping that wasn't the decision you'd make."

I suck in a breath. "You want me to stay with you?"

His face softens, like he's now more at ease. "Of course, I do."

I stare down at his hand—something about it screams ownership. "Do you think Dallas will be okay with that? Having me there while he's grieving?"

Maybe I can convince him to stay at the bed and breakfast with me.

"I think he might enjoy the company, but if you don't feel comfortable, it's okay. You'll have to stay at the bed and breakfast by yourself, though."

I'm caught off guard. "What? Why?"

"If I sleep there with you, people will know something is going on between us, and we can't let your dirty little secret out, can we?"

His voice changes with those last words.

The mood shifts.

My decision to fake date Eli haunts me again.

HUDSON'S SISTER, Lauren, picks us up from the airport. To say I'm a nervous wreck to meet his family is an understatement. The entire flight was spent debating with myself on whether I made the right decision in coming.

Willow never questioned me when I asked her to book us a flight. No one has told Tillie, but I have a feeling she'll throw something when she finds out. Hopefully, she's too busy making someone else's life miserable than to worry about mine right now.

Hudson carries our bags when we land as I follow him through an airport that's definitely not LAX. A petite, dark-haired woman wearing scrubs is leaning against a pink Mustang. I recognize her from Dallas's Instagram.

"Flying private, huh?" she asks, pushing herself off the car. "Small-town boy is turning into Mr. Big Shot."

"Nice to see you too, baby sister," Hudson replies, giving her a hug. "I told you not to drive the Pink Panther and take Mom's car. It's too small for three people."

She squints at him. "First off, her name isn't Pink Panther, and had I driven Mom's car, I would have been late picking your ungrateful ass up. My work hours are nuts, and I couldn't even get off early when I found out about Lucy."

We all flinch at her last statement.

Hudson's hand tightens around the handle of my Louis Vuitton luggage. "You need to quit that fucking job then. That's bullshit."

Color rises in her cheeks. She looks almost sleep deprived.

"I can't quit my job because I have bills and an ass-load of student loans to pay off for the half Mom and Dad aren't paying." She walks to the back of the car and pops the trunk. "Unless you hit the lottery and want to pay them?"

"We both wish," he mutters, placing our bags in the trunk.

Her face is blank when she shoves her hand my way. "I'm Lauren."

I shake it. "Stella. Thank you for picking us up."

Her lips tilt up into a fake smile.

Is she upset about Lucy or mad I tagged along?

Hudson slams the trunk closed. "I'll take the back seat. Stella, you can have the front."

"No," I rush out. "I'll take the back. You two probably have a lot to talk about."

"We're going to be in the same vehicle. I can talk to her from the back."

The next five minutes is spent arguing about who will take what seat until Lauren threatens to leave us at the airport.

I lose.

"FYI, you look like shit, Hudson," she says.

Hudson smacks the back of her seat. "You're so sweet. How are you holding up?"

I look over at her as a tear slips down her cheek.

She wipes it away as though it never happened. "As good as I can be. Lucy was so young. It's unfair."

I nod in agreement but don't feel comfortable enough to join the conversation.

"And Dallas?" Hudson asks.

"Not good. He's holding in the hurt to be strong for Maven, but it won't help him in the long run. You need to talk to him."

"You know how Dallas is. Us Barnes boys don't like to talk about feelings. We feel like pussies."

"Don't undermine pussies. They're very powerful," Lauren argues. "If he'll open up to anyone, it will be you."

Hudson runs his hand over his puffy face. "I'll try."

Lauren looks over at me. "Did you ever meet Lucy?"

I nod. "She was very sweet."

She smiles at my answer.

Lauren's attention goes to the road, but I can tell she's skeptical of my presence.

THE RIDE IS LONG, and I yawn when I see the welcome sign to Blue Beech.

"Holy shit, you weren't joking about it being in the middle of nowhere," I comment.

"Welcome to Blue Beech," Lauren replies. "Where there's no fancy coffee shops or malls to buy designer handbags."

Definitely skeptical.

Perfect.

"Lauren," Hudson scolds.

She rolls her eyes and goes silent.

Hudson's attention turns to me. "There's not much when you first get to town, but it gets better. The circle is where people hang out, and the excitement happens."

Lauren scoffs. "It sounds like you're trying to sell Blue Beech to her."

Hudson ignores her while I keep my thoughts to myself and stare out the window. Buildings come into view. People are walking around downtown and sitting on benches. Quaint shops and restaurants line the streets. We drive out of town and onto country roads until she pulls into the drive of a ranch home. The landscaping boasts bright flowers with dozens of gnomes arranged between them.

"This is my parents' house," Hudson tells me.

"MOM AND DAD, THIS IS STELLA," Hudson introduces.

Their house is as adorable inside as it is out.

It's cozy. Family pictures are everywhere. The furniture is worn but still cared for.

"And Stella, these are my parents," he goes on. "Rory and John."

I give them a shy wave.

Me shy?

That's unusual.

"It's nice to meet you," I say. "I'm sorry for your loss."

Rory gives me a small smile. I have a feeling I'll be seeing a lot of those here. They don't want to be rude but are mourning.

"Thank you," Rory says. "We appreciate you coming and giving Dallas time off so he could be with Lucy."

You can tell Rory is a nice woman by just looking at her. Her brown hair is pulled back into a chignon, and she's wearing a purple tunic and black leggings.

John resembles an older version of Dallas and Hudson. He's tall, his hair similar to his sons, with speckles of gray throughout the strands. I have no doubt he was as handsome as them growing up.

"You're welcome. I was happy to help," I answer.

My financial advisor suggested against me covering Lucy's medical bills. I make good money, but I'm not loaded. Maybe to other people I am, but in the world I live in, I'm just comfortable. You decide what you want to spend your money on, and I decided I wanted to help the guy who looked out for me for years. I didn't want him worrying about finances during this difficult time.

"What's happening with sleeping arrangements?" Rory asks.

Hudson and I exchange a look.

"We're staying at Dallas's," he answers.

"*Both of you?*" Lauren questions.

"Yes, both of us. She's comfortable with us." Hudson arches a brow. "Unless you want to give up your bed? I wouldn't mind sleeping in your apartment."

"You can have the couch," she fires back.

"It will be good for Dallas to have company," John cuts in. Wrinkles crease his forehead when he frowns. "I hope he doesn't take it as hard as I think he will. There's no coming back from losing the woman you love. I pray to God I go before your mother does."

Rory reaches down and grabs his hand.

Oh, hell. I'm witnessing a love story.

People really act like this in real life?

CHAPTER TWENTY-EIGHT

Hudson

DALLAS'S front door is unlocked.

Stella stayed at my parents' while I took the eight-minute drive to his house. I want to see where he's at in his head before anything else.

He's sitting on the leather couch with his head bowed when I walk into the living room. He doesn't look up until I beat my boots against the wood floor. He stares at me blankly with loose shoulders. His eyes are red and underlined with dark circles. He's been waiting for this moment. The moment to release his pain in privacy.

I feel like shit for interrupting.

"Where's Maven?" I ask.

He rubs one eye and then the other. "Taking a nap."

"Have you told her?"

He nods. "This morning. We've been in here all day watching her favorite movies." He squeezes his eyes shut. "The ones she and Lucy watched all the time. It seems to be helping her take her mind off it temporarily, but I know it won't fix it." His voice breaks. "My girl lost her mother, and I don't know how I'm going to raise her alone."

"You know all of us will be here to help you every step of the way. You're an amazing father." I sit next to him and wrap my arm around his shoulders. "Lucy will never be replaceable to Maven, but Mom and Lauren will do everything they can to help."

"You don't understand," his voice falls into a sob. "I thought I prepared myself to lose her, but I was so damn wrong. I was never ready for this. Nothing can stop this pain. I loved her more than I loved my own life."

I fight back my tears. "None of us were ready to lose her."

"Lauren was working at the hospital when it happened."

"Were you there?"

He nods. "I've been there every minute of the day. Mom has been watching Maven for me. Without my family, I couldn't have even made it this far."

"We'll always be here for you. You call, I'll come running."

He glances over at me with his shoulders still slumped. "You staying here while you're home?"

"You know I am." I pause. "Is it okay if Stella does too?"

He flinches. "She couldn't find someone to cover your job?"

"We didn't bother trying. She asked to come with me."

He tilts his head to the side. "That's nice of her. I know Lucy appreciated everything she did for us."

"I can have her stay at Mom and Dad's if you want."

He raises a brow. "Does she want to stay here with you?"

I shrug. "She'll probably feel more comfortable here with us, but if you want privacy, Mom and Dad won't mind her crashing in my old bedroom."

"She can stay here. Maven likes her. She thinks she's a big shot for hanging out with someone on TV, so maybe it'll get her mind on something else. She can have the guest room, so you can either sleep on the couch up here or on the one in the basement."

"You know I'm a gentleman."

He scoffs. "That's not what Grady has been going around saying after your little alley talk."

I flinch hearing that bastard's name. "He deserved that and more."

"I hear ya."

DALLAS WAS right about Stella helping Maven.

Maven has spent the evening showing Stella her bedroom and doll collection. They then watched TV until Maven crashed out on the couch, and Dallas carried his daughter to her bed.

"Everything good?" I ask Stella, guiding her down the stairs that leads to the basement.

She sighs. "Yes, I just hate how bad I am with people who are sad. I feel shy around your family, like an outsider, and I don't want them to think I'm bitchy."

"Don't think like that. It takes a lot for my family not to like someone, let alone call them bitchy. They appreciate everything you've done for our family and have liked you since before you even got here."

"Your mom asked me to help bake for the reception. I've never baked anything in my life and will definitely be the joke of the town when she tells people I don't know the difference between flour and sugar. They'll tell you to kick me to the curb."

I grab her waist and pull her to me. "My ex couldn't cook for shit. As long as you make me happy, and *definitely* as long as you keep riding my dick like you do, I could give two fucks if you know how to bake a pie. You don't have to be anyone else to get the approval of me or my family."

"What about your sister? She's not my biggest fan."

It looks like I wasn't the only one to notice Lauren's apprehension toward Stella. I make a note to talk to her.

"Lauren means well. She just doesn't want to see me get hurt again."

"I won't hurt you," she whispers. "So please do the same for me."

I grab her chin with the tip of my finger and drag it up. "Stella, I have no idea what the fuck is going on between us, or where it will go, but I'll do everything in my power never to hurt you."

CHAPTER TWENTY-NINE

Stella

LUCY'S WAKE IS TODAY.

I've never been to one before and wasn't sure what to expect when I got dressed this morning. I want to make a good impression on Hudson's family in case they ever find out about us.

We're at the funeral home, and I'm standing next to Hudson while receiving every odd look known to man. Nosy stares. Dirty looks. Friendly smiles.

I introduce myself as Dallas's friend, and a few parents have scolded their children for asking for my autograph. I don't mind it. The only times I have is when they do it to sell it online and make a profit.

Dallas and Maven have sat next to Lucy's casket all day, and my heart breaks for them. You can see the love he had for his wife everywhere on him.

"Heads-up," Hudson says. "My ex just arrived."

He tilts his head toward a blonde walking in with a cute guy.

"The cheating ex?" I ask.

It's a stupid question since he's only had one ex, but her showing up takes me by surprise.

"Yep," he clips out.

"And the best friend?"

"That would be him."

I wish jealousy wasn't creeping through me like a bad drug as I study her. She's pretty, in shape, and I'm sure doesn't have an unhealthy relationship with carbs like I do. Cameron has the all-American girl look complete with the blond hair, large bust, and tan, toned legs.

I should walk over and thank her, maybe slip her a hundred, for letting Hudson go. If she didn't cheat on him, he wouldn't be with me. She would be the one receiving the attention I'm growing addicted to. I force myself to move my focus from her to the dickhead friend. Dude is attractive with blond hair, decent-size muscles, and a cute smile, but he's no Hudson.

"FYI, you're so much hotter than him," I whisper, looping my arm through Hudson's. "Talk about a downgrade."

He peeks down at our connection. "Appreciate it, Hollywood."

We've never touched like this in public. He waited until everyone was asleep before getting in bed with me last night.

I wait to see if he pulls away and smile when he doesn't. Hudson has no problem showing ownership with me. I'm the one who's scared … and stopping it because of my Eli situation.

"You don't think she's going to come over here, do you?" I ask.

"Doubt it. The last time she and Grady came around me, my hand ended up around his neck."

"Yeah, let's hope they stick to their side," I mutter.

I'M WASHING my hands when I hear the bathroom door slam shut after Hudson's ex walks in.

"Stella, right?" she asks.

She smiles and waves. It's not a genuine smile, more along

the lines of one that says she wants to kill me and hide me in these cornfields kind of smile.

It won't make a good impression on Hudson's family and the good people of Blue Beech if I have a girl fight in the bathroom at a funeral.

I grab a paper towel and dry my hands. "It is."

"Everyone keeps saying how nice it was for you to come all this way for Dallas. I mean, you were only his employer. Are you this nice to everyone who works for you?" She blows out a breath. "Must be exhausting."

Really? This is the route she's going?

"Dallas was my bodyguard for years, and I got to know him and his family, so yes, I care about the people who work for me."

She straightens her stance, and her glossy lips slip into a hard line. "How do you and Hudson know each other?"

Chick is trying to trap me.

Like me, she's wearing a dress and heels, so if she does try to fight me, I might have a chance. I've managed to master living in heels. I can squat in these bad boys, run from men with cameras, and I've even boxed in them a few times for a commercial. I'll be able to hold my own on this one.

Hopefully.

"Hudson is working for me now," I answer, giving her a satisfied smile. "He took Dallas's job."

Yep, he's with me every night.

"How kind of him." She lets out a bitter laugh and moves away from the door. "You want to know something hilarious? Hudson used to give Dallas so much shit for working for you and constantly told him to quit. I recall him calling you a spoiled diva once, but he's a good brother, so I'm sure he'll do the job until he comes home. You do know he will always come home, right?"

Her words make me light-headed, and I'm thankful she's no longer blocking the door.

Who starts shit at a funeral?

I shrug. "I guess he changed his mind. He seems to be pretty good at it. Maybe it's his calling."

She scowls. "Doubt it."

I give her a forced smile, turn around, and leave the room.

"CAN I SHOW YOU AROUND TOWN?" Hudson asks when we walk out of the funeral home. His hand goes to my back as he guides me down the sidewalk. "We can grab a cupcake from Magnolia's Bakery or a sandwich at the diner?"

I look around. "Are you sure that's a good idea, given all the curious eyes?"

"They'll think I'm being a gentleman and keeping you company."

"What about Dallas?"

"He and Maven are meeting with the pastor. Dallas is unsure of the best approach to explain everything to Maven. She knows her mom is gone, but he wants to make sure she knows Lucy is in heaven."

"Poor thing. I can't even imagine what she's going through right now."

"Maven is strong like her mother."

There's a pause of silence.

It's broken when he claps his hands. "So … how about that cupcake?"

I smile. "Only if you help me work off the calories later."

"You fucking know it."

People stop us to hug Hudson and welcome him home when we walk down a sidewalk lined with beautiful flowers. They express their sympathy for his loss and then introduce themselves to me. They're all friendly. Blue Beech is nothing like LA.

Hudson points out all the landmarks and the spots where he and his friends caused the most trouble. He tells me about his bright idea to toilet paper the gazebo for their senior prank that resulted in him being busted. His punishment was giving manicures at the local nursing home. We end our tour by stopping at a shop with a bright yellow door.

A bell rings when we walk in, and the small space is crowded with tables. It smells like heaven and calories. You walk in and know you'll be leaving the place ten pounds heavier.

"Holy shit," I say as we make our way toward the glass counter filled with cupcakes galore. "I want one of everything."

Hudson laughs. "I can make that happen."

A middle-aged woman wearing a bright pink floral apron with streaks of icing on it grins from behind the counter. "I knew you couldn't come home and resist one of my red velvet cupcakes. Now, honey, I know you've been hearing condolences all day, so I'm going to let my sweets do the talking for me." She turns around and grabs a large box of cupcakes. "I planned on dropping these off at your brother's after I close, but I might as well give them to you while you're here. Give these to Dallas and that angel of his. I don't mind if you snag a few for yourself."

Hudson takes the box from her with a smile. "Will do, Maggie. Appreciate it. You know how much Maven loves your shop."

Maggie looks over at me. "And what can I get you, sweetie?"

There are so many options.

I wasn't hungry ten minutes ago, but my stomach suddenly growls.

"What do you suggest?"

She points at Hudson. "The Barnes men seem to have a weakness for my red velvet, but I have a new strawberry cupcake that's been quite the hit lately."

"Strawberry it is then."

Hudson pays for our cupcakes, and we sit at a table next to the window.

"Why is everyone so nice around here?" I whisper.

He chuckles, looking proud. "It's Blue Beech. We have each

other's backs, know what kind of cupcakes our friends like when they're having a bad day, and are always up for giving a helping hand."

"It's so different than what I'm used to."

"You grew up in LA, right?"

I nod. "My mom knew she wanted me to be famous before I left her womb, and where else but California can that be accomplished?"

"California is all you know. Blue Beech is all I know. You become familiar and comfortable with your surroundings."

"I wish I'd grown up in a place like this."

He winks. "We accept newcomers of all ages if you ever want to make a life change. It's a good place to raise a family."

His response is my cue to dig into my cupcake. Maggie was right. The strawberry is to die for.

"It's where you want to raise your family, isn't it?" I ask, licking frosting from my thumb.

"Wouldn't want to be anywhere else. You want to raise yours in LA?"

"I never really thought about having kids."

"You don't want to be a mother?"

I shrug. "I'm not sure I'd know how to be one." I lower my voice. "I'm scared I'll be a terrible one."

He looks shocked at my admission. "Why would you think that?"

"I never had a good example."

"So? Trust me, when that day comes, you'll have that maternal instinct. I know it. You will be one incredible mom, Stella."

"Let's hope so."

I realized my mother wanted me only as an opportunity years ago. I saw the way Knox's mom used him for money. The same thing happened to countless friends of mine in the business. Our parents don't care. Some, like my mom, saw us as meal tickets, and others threw money at their kids as an excuse to get out of parenting.

He reaches over and brushes his thumb over my lip to wipe away the frosting. “Goddamn, I wish I could’ve used my tongue to clean that off instead.”

CHAPTER THIRTY

Hudson

DALLAS LEANS BACK in his chair and rests his arms behind his neck. "When were you going to tell me you're sleeping with Stella?"

We're back at his place, and our family left an hour ago. Maven is spending the night with my parents. Stella is in the shower. And we're in the kitchen reminiscing about the good times we had with Lucy over beers.

I take a long drink before answering, "I have no idea what you're talking about."

"Don't bullshit me. I'm a grieving man. I deserve the truth. You took her around town—"

"That means I'm fucking her?" I interrupt.

"No, but the way you look at each other does. For fuck's sake, you brought her home with you, she has you doing yoga, and who knows what else. You're fucking her."

I rub my temples. "You have too much shit going on right now to worry about my sex life. Hell, I'm more worried about you being okay than my sex life. My concern right now is you, how you're doing, and what I can do to help you through this. We can talk about who I'm sticking my dick into another time."

Preferably never.

Kissing, or fucking, and telling isn't my thing. I lost my virginity before all my friends. Hell, before Dallas, but no one knew because I don't have a big-ass mouth. I would listen to the guys in the locker room bragging about getting to third base when I was hitting home runs. I've never felt the need to brag and never wanted to disrespect Cameron.

"Appreciate it, brother, but I feel like all I've done today is talk about my feelings and thank people for their condolences. I don't want fucking condolences. I don't want pity. I don't want fucking cupcakes. I just want my wife back." He looks up at the ceiling, shaking his head, and tries to hide the tears I know are impending. "She was perfect. The best wife a man could ask for. An amazing mother, beautiful, caring. Why? Why, Hudson? Why did God have to take her away from me? Why? I needed her! I loved her!"

I rub my eyes to stop my tears. I wish I was better with words, but I'll give it a shot. "I know you loved Lucy, and she loved you. You had a love stronger than anything I've ever seen. She had love before she passed. Her heart was full because you gave her a great life. She was happy and knew you'd be a great dad to Maven." My heart slams against my chest. "I'm glad we're talking about this. Everyone has been afraid of you holding it in."

He scoffs. "Who are you now? Counselor Hudson?"

"You can't always be the strong one." I pull myself up from my chair and grab us another round of beers before handing him one. "More to take the edge off."

He draws in a deep breath and uses the back of his hand to wipe his eyes. "Thanks, man." He takes a drink and sighs. "You and Stella, huh?"

I rub my hands down my pants. "You pissed about it?"

"No, more along the lines of surprised."

I raise a brow. "Surprised she would mess around with someone like me?"

"Fuck no. I'm surprised you opened up your mind to see her

for who she really is." He tips his beer toward me. "I told you it was a good idea to go there. You owe me."

"Yeah, yeah, I'll do a load of your laundry or some shit."

"You still quitting when they find someone else to take the job?"

I run a hand through my hair. Stella and I haven't had this conversation yet, but I know I don't want to stay in California. "That's my plan."

"What are you doing then?" His voice turns harsh. "You're just going to leave her? Why are you leading her on if you're not staying?"

"We're *fucking,* Dallas. Having fun. Not getting married. She's not going to give up her life. I'm not giving up mine."

His eyes harden. "You've had that talk then? You've explained that under no circumstances are you staying there?"

"Kind of."

I've told her I'd never leave Blue Beech. Isn't that enough?

"Fucking liar."

I GO DOWN to the basement in search of Stella when Dallas goes to bed.

I find her standing in front of the bathroom vanity looking in the mirror with her back to me. She's running her hands through her wet hair. I sneak up behind her, circle my arms around her hips, and slowly dust kisses along her neck. She tilts her head to the side, and I take that as an invitation for more.

I'm wrong.

My hands fall to my sides when she pulls away and leaves the bathroom.

"What's wrong?" I ask, following her into the bedroom.

She starts looking through her suitcase. "Nothing." She picks up a shirt, then drops it.

"Don't bullshit me, Stella. If I did something to piss you off, tell me so I can fix it."

I don't do the whole beating around the bush shit, and I think Stella had a habit of doing that in her last relationship. I want us to be up-front, open, and personal.

I grab her hand and turn her around to face me, and her attention goes to the floor.

"This isn't the right place to have this conversation, Hudson."

I get that. She wants to be respectful and not argue in Dallas's home. I respect her for respecting him.

I tug on her hand and start walking toward the stairs. "Come on, then."

"What?"

"We're going for a drive."

"Now?"

I nod. "My truck is here. I'll even buy you an ice cream cone if we make it to the shop in time."

A tiny smile breaks through her lips. "Jesus, you and your sweets. If I stay here any longer, my ass will get even bigger."

"I like that."

I KILL the engine to my truck when we make it to our destination—Blue Beech Edge River. It's my favorite spot in town to come and think. It's also the choice spot for horny teenagers who have nowhere else to go to get laid.

I flip on the overhead light and look at her. "Tell me what I did."

She sighs, waving her hand through the air, and a light blush passes over her cheeks. This isn't a conversation she's ready to have. "You know what? It's not even that important. Let's get that ice cream, and we'll talk about it another time."

She's shutting down on me.

"It is fucking important if you're upset about it. Tell me if I did something wrong, so I won't do it again."

"I overheard your conversation with Dallas," she whispers.

I pause and go through what we talked about in the kitchen, but I'm drawing a blank on what could've offended her. "And you're pissed at me why?"

Her gaze drops down to her lap before she starts to answer, but I interrupt her.

"We're not talking about shit until you look at me. Don't hide. Tell me how to fix this. If I did something stupid, don't let me get away with it."

She glances up at me, and my stomach twists when I see the sadness in her eyes.

"You told him we're pretty much fuck buddies and you're bailing as soon as your time is up." She shakes her head, and her voice breaks. "What are we doing, Hudson? Am I only a good time to you? Some rebound to mend your broken heart?"

Fuck.

This is all my fault.

I slap the steering wheel. "No, Stella. You aren't a rebound or a fling that doesn't mean anything to me. Am I confused? Hell yes. You know I don't like to share, and if you say the word, I'll make you mine right now. If you say you're mine, we'll figure out a plan to make it work with us. Until then, I'm sorry, but I can't plan a future with a woman who won't even claim me. That's why I fought this in the beginning because I was scared of this happening."

"So am I!" she screams. "I never expected to fall for you like this. I'm scared your feelings aren't as strong as mine and terrified of dropping my career and risking everything only for you to walk away from me. You recently got out of a long-term relationship that lasted over a decade. How can I be certain I'm not a rebound … a fuck buddy …"

"I have the same uncertainties, Hollywood. We've had long-term relationships that failed and are scared of getting our hearts shattered again. I won't deny I'm afraid, but that also doesn't mean I'm against falling in love again." I make sure we have good eye contact before continuing. "In fact, I know I'm not." I press my hand to my chest over my heart. "I can already feel you inside me, repairing the parts Cameron broke, and I'm afraid you'll do even more damage."

I'm shocked at my honesty. I don't open up. I'm not an emotional dude.

She swipes a tear from her cheek. "I'm so afraid of getting hurt. I told myself I was anti-relationship because the heartache, the loss, it's just too much for me."

"Looks like we're just two complicated souls looking for love."

She keeps crying.

"Come here, Hollywood." I grab her arm to drag her onto my lap and start brushing away the tears until there's none left. "I don't want to make you cry. I told you, I'll do everything in my power never to hurt you, but I want the same from you. Take this step with me. Go all in. Stop pretending to be with another man."

She shivers, her body shaking, when I run my hands down her arms.

"I want you to be mine. It killed me yesterday when I couldn't hold your hand—couldn't touch you in fear of what your consequences would be. Goddamn, you have no idea how hard that's killing me. I'm over here falling for a woman I can't claim."

She's breathing heavily while staring down at me with dilated pupils and starts trembling in my arms.

"I want that too," she whispers.

"Promise me you'll do something about it … that you'll do whatever it takes to be mine. Tell me you're ready to be all in."

She nods repeatedly. "I promise. All in."

I can feel her heart beating as she presses her chest into me and rests her lips on mine.

"Now claim me, Hudson Barnes."

CHAPTER THIRTY-ONE

Stella

I ASKED him to claim me.

That's what he does.

His hand curls around the back of my head, and I waste no time devouring his mouth. This is the most intimate kiss we've shared. Something about confessing our feelings and telling each other we don't want to walk away seems to have made everything so much hotter.

Every touch more exciting.

I tilt my head to the side, exposing my bare neck and silently pleading for more of anything he's willing to give.

Touch me. Kiss me. Love me.

I shiver when his lips hit my neck, sucking hard on my sensitive skin, and I know I'm going to be covering up the evidence of his mouth there with makeup tomorrow.

He's so addictive.

"Say you're mine," he gasps. "All fucking mine."

"I'm yours," I moan. "Only yours."

The space is small, but I manage to get his pants down far enough to pull his cock free. I scoot back to get a good grip and slowly stroke him. He pushes my dress up past my breasts, massaging them and pinching a nipple that nearly sends me over the edge, and swipes my panties to the side before slowly lowering me onto him. The rough texture of the steering wheel bites into my back when I grind down on his lap and take in his length.

I lose control as soon as I start riding him, giving him my all, and he grabs my hips, slamming me into him with more power.

The sound of our heavy breathing and skin slapping takes over the silent cab. The aroma of our sex fills up the small space.

I've made up my mind by the time my orgasm shakes through me.

I'm willing to take the risk.

I'm ready to make Hudson Barnes mine.

I just have to figure out how.

I STRETCH my arms out against the crisp sheets and feel the emptiness in the spot next to me.

I decided to stay behind for Lucy's funeral today. It's too intimate for an outsider and would make people curious. I've been followed for the past decade and had friends sell stories on me to make a quick buck, so I'm not the most trusting person. Trust isn't just given. It has to be earned.

I stretch my arm out to grab my phone from the nightstand, and there's a Post-it note stuck to the screen.

Coffee maker is on.

All the necessary ingredients to make it your own are in the kitchen.

Call or text if you need anything.

Later, you're mine.

Hudson

He must have gone to the grocery store early this morning while I was sleeping and got coconut milk because I don't recall seeing any yesterday. He has to be exhausted. We went for round two when we got back last night, and I couldn't feel my legs by the time he rolled off me, took me in his arms, and we fell asleep. He didn't have one nightmare.

I get out of my bed to brush my teeth and head upstairs to the kitchen in search of the coffee maker.

It's on.

Thank God.

It's embarrassing, but I have no idea how to make coffee. I give myself a mental note to watch a YouTube video on it. You can learn how to do anything on the internet—cook, clean, steal cars, make coffee. Ah, modern technology.

I'm about to start my coffee-making research when a close-up of Willow's face pops up on my phone screen. My stomach tenses for some reason. I'm scared it's bad news, and bad news before your first cup of coffee is the worst way to start the day. I'm not ready to adult or have conversations until at least my second.

Please be a checkup call or an update on a new audition.

Not something that's going to turn my life upside down, or Tillie's reaction to my mini-vacation with another man.

I put the call on speaker. "Hello?"

"What the hell is wrong with you?" she yells on the other line. "Are you trying to commit career suicide, you lunatic?"

"Huh?" is the only response I can muster out while I run through the possible scenarios of what she could be mad about.

"Everyone and their mama are calling you a cheater right now. It's everywhere. Someone sold a video of you dry humping *or possibly fucking* Hudson, you can't really tell from the angle, in the front seat of a pickup truck. The internet is blowing up!"

Fuck me. Fuck me. This is the end of my career.

My throat tightens, my stomach revolts, and fear snakes through me. I never thought news would travel like that here, or that someone would follow us in order to sell a story. Hell, I thought we were in the boondocks of fucking nowhere.

"Tell me you're joking," I stutter out, my throat tightening as tears build at my eyes. "Tell me this is some prank you're playing on me."

"Tough shit, Stella. It's not a joke. It's code red. Code fucking red."

"Who … who could've done this?"

"I'm assuming paparazzi got word that you took a flight there and decided to meander to good ole Iowa to see if they could stalk you and find a story."

The tears start to fall. I was too careless, acting too free, and not thinking about the damage that kissing Hudson would do to my career.

"What do I do, Willow?"

I cringe when I see a call beeping in from Tillie. I hit ignore. The witch is going to have to wait to rip my head off.

"You need to come clean. Tell the truth about Eli."

"Do you know the damage that'll do to my reputation?"

"Uh, probably nothing near as bad as looking like an unfaithful tramp."

"I have to talk to Eli … to Hudson … before I do anything."

"Do that and get back with me ASAP. I need to put out a statement before this snowballs. In the meantime, quit being so damn dumb."

"You're the one who told me to start banging Hudson!"

"Really? I also told you to bang Justin Timberlake when he was single, but did you try to jump on that shit? I'm all for you being happy, girlfriend, and this little selling your soul deal isn't making you happy. The problem now is saving your ass. They can sue you. It's breach of contract." She pauses. "There's more."

As if this day couldn't get any fucking worse.

"What now?" I burst out.

"Spencer Marcum is also making headlines."

"I should care why?"

"Not only are the headlines blazing with pictures of you and Hudson but they're also talking about you and Spencer. He did an interview with Howard Stern and said you cheated on Knox with him."

My head starts spinning, and my heart drops to my stomach. I'm going to lose the two most important things in my life in one day. My career and Hudson. I run to the bathroom and start to dry heave, but nothing comes out.

"I'm going to lose him," I whisper when I gain control of myself, tears blinding me.

"What?" she asks.

"Hudson. I'm going to lose him. He'll hate me when he finds out I cheated on Knox."

"Why? It was before him."

"He hates cheaters, despises them, and thinks once a cheater, always a cheater."

"Explain the situation. He'll understand." Her voice is tight. She's pissed at me but still has my back.

"He won't," I sob. "He won't understand."

CHAPTER THIRTY-TWO

Hudson

FUNERALS.

I hate them.

And I fucking hate the fact that I've gone to my fair share of them. They never get easier. What makes them even worse is when they're for someone who was taken too soon.

When someone dies at ninety-five, people go on about their victory of making it so far.

She almost made it a century. She was badass. What was her secret?

When someone dies at thirty, it's a tragedy.

The only question is why.

Why were they taken away so soon? Why couldn't we have them longer?

The world is not fucking fair. Death isn't fucking fair. The grim reaper always seems to come for the good ones—the ones with hearts of gold who are supposed to stay with us until their skin wrinkles, until they get dentures, until they get the chance to spoil their grandchildren.

Sadness gnaws at me stronger with every passing tear. I peek over at Dallas sitting a few seats down from me with Maven settled on his lap. His arms are enveloped around her like a shield, and they stare at the purple casket topped with flowers and lined with gold trim, both of their eyes swollen. He's still fighting to hold it together for Maven and to be a strong father. I think back to what Lauren said. She was right. It's all an act.

This is a reminder that I need to grab life by the balls and take advantage of every day I'm given. Every single fucking second of my life needs to matter because I don't know how many more I'll get. I can't keep burying parts of me away from Stella in fear of the future because hell, who knows how long mine will be.

Dallas takes Maven up with him when he gives the eulogy. He squeezes her hand, and the words slip from his mouth slowly. He's composing himself the best he can while reminding us what a good woman Lucy was. Even though none of us need reminded.

My mother is crying next to me. She's lost a daughter. Her son lost a wife. Her granddaughter is now motherless. Every person in this room is losing a sliver of their heart today.

I wish Stella was here, but I understand her reasoning. I tip my head down as tears fall from my cheeks while silently asking God not to take anyone else from me.

I THROW my arm around Dallas's shoulders as people clear out of the funeral home. "I'm here for you, brother. You and Maven, whatever you need, you let me know."

He wipes his dark eyes. "Lucy's death has forced me to give up on having any certainty in this life except for one—that I can rely on my family every minute of every day, no matter what. All of you are the only reason I'm standing today and not breaking down in front of my daughter. I'll never be able to thank you guys enough. And what you did, taking that job so I could spend Lucy's last few weeks by her side, I'll never be able to repay you for that."

I squeeze his shoulder. "Family doesn't ever need to repay

family for helping them. We'll always be here, come hell or high water … or Hollywood."

I get a small chuckle from him.

"I'll be at your side every step of the way. You can count on that."

I don't know where we'll go from here, but I can't hang out with Stella in clubs when my family is broken thousands of miles away.

I have a decision to make.

And it won't be an easy one.

I'M THE SUGAR-RUNNER.

Not only does my mother love to bake, she loves to emotional bake. If she's having a bad day, she's in the kitchen making something. It's her happy place.

The reception is being held at my parents', and I know it will smell like the Pillsbury Doughboy's ass crack when I get there. The kitchen was already loaded with pies, cakes, and cookies this morning. No doubt there will be more.

My mom left the funeral home as soon as the service ended without making small talk or thanking people for coming like we did. She wanted everything in order so Dallas wouldn't stress about it. She stopped to pick up Stella before going home, and I'm meeting them at her house.

Thinking back to the conversation I had with Stella last night brings a smile to my face. She's going to end that bullshit agreement with Eli. We'll figure out a way to make our relationship work.

I toss every item on my mom's list into the shopping cart and head to the only open checkout lane. People stop me on my way to express their condolences. Everyone loved Lucy. She didn't have a bad bone in her body. She was a pharmacy tech at our local drug store and always went out of her way to help people. She even dropped prescriptions off at people's houses if they were too sick to pick them up. Everyone is going to miss her.

Mrs. Pipes shoots me a friendly wave while the cashier finishes helping her, and I begin loading my groceries on the belt. When I finish, I grab my phone to check for missed calls, and something catches my eye before I turn the screen on.

The air grows thin.

My vision grows blurry, and I feel like I've been punched in the stomach.

Stella has graced tabloid covers for as long as I can remember. I never paid attention before—only briefly noticing her name because my brother worked for her.

Until now.

My muscles painfully tick underneath my skin as I read the headline again, just in case my mind is fucking with me. I blink, giving myself one more opportunity to act like I didn't read it correctly. I lose again and clench my jaw while taking in the words written above a photo of Stella kissing me while straddling my lap in my pickup.

Stella Mendes busted cheating on Eli with bodyguard! It's not the first time it's happened! See her many scandals with other men, including actor Spencer Marcum!

What fucking creep spied on us to take this picture?

This headline has to be bullshit, right?

They need catchy yet false headlines to make sales.

My fingers twitch with desperation to pick up the magazine and buy it, but word will be all over town if someone catches me. I snatch it from the holder and flip through the pages until I find the story about Stella … and me. I take pictures of each page with my phone and put the magazine back as soon as Mrs. Pipes wheels away her cart.

"I take it your mother is on a baking spree?" Jojo asks when she starts to ring me up.

I graduated with her, and her dad owns the grocery store. She's also one of Cameron's friends.

I force a smile. "How could you tell?"

"Poor Dallas. If you guys need anything else, call me and I'll drop it off after my shift, okay? It's no hassle."

"I'll let her know. Thanks."

I pay, grab the bags, and am about to walk out when Jojo stops me.

"Hudson, I want you to know I had no idea what was going on with Cameron and Grady."

I shrug. "It happened. I'm over it."

I could give two shits about Cameron right now. All that's on my mind is Stella.

I throw the groceries in the passenger seat and pull my phone from my pocket as soon as I slam the door shut. I can't believe I'm reading tabloid stories about my girlfriend … or the girl I'm screwing … because I'm not sure what she is to me. I *really* can't believe they have pictures of me in there.

Damn, how my life has changed.

I don't like it one fucking bit.

Don't like my business out there like this.

I sit in my truck for a good fifteen minutes reading the article about us having some sordid affair behind Eli's back. That's not the worst part. There are also claims that our affair isn't the first one she's had.

Spencer Marcum, another actor, let it slip that he slept with her when she was with Knox. He has the texts to prove it, and they're posted on the next page.

She asked him not to say anything to Knox or anyone else and said it could never happen again. She texted him again a week later with a heads-up that she told Knox out of guilt, and Knox said he better not see him around.

Who was this woman? It's not my Stella.

I shake my head, gritting my teeth. I've fallen for another liar. Another fraud. *Another cheater.*

I close out of the pictures and open my browser to search for other stories about her and Spencer online. There are pages of them dating back to over a year ago. It's been a while since their supposed hookup happened, but I hate the fact that she never told me about this after knowing how I despise cheaters.

She's just like Cameron.

I can't have my heart broken again by someone who doesn't cherish commitment.

Me: What do you know about Stella and Spencer Marcum?

I'm an asshole for even bringing this up to him today.

Dallas: Not my story to tell, man.

I want to tell him it is because he's my brother, but the last thing he needs to worry about is my relationship problems. He would've told me if it wasn't true, and he didn't.

Not my story to tell means it happened, but he doesn't know all the details, or doesn't care to share Stella's business.

CHAPTER THIRTY-THREE

Stella

"IF YOU'LL SET the timer on the oven for fifteen minutes, we can start on the next batch," Rory instructs while handing me the pan of unbaked cookies we made from scratch.

She also showed me how to make a cherry pie and chocolate chip cookies.

All in a two-hour span.

I haven't baked this much in my entire life.

She left the funeral early and stopped to ask if I'd like to help her get everything prepared for the reception. Even though I'm a nervous wreck on the verge of losing everything I love and have been dodging every phone call coming through for the past few hours, I couldn't say no to her. So here I am, baking cookies while on the edge of falling into a full panic attack at the thought of Hudson leaving me. I'm playing Betty Crocker while my career is going up in flames.

Just wonderful.

Hudson doesn't read the tabloids, so there's a chance he might not find out that not only is my career going down the drain but his name is also being dragged into the gutter with it. It's wrong for me to even consider hiding this from him, but I'm not sure what else to do.

Rory is helping take my mind off my problems while she tells me story after story of how she and John fell in love in high school and raised their children in this house. They've been married for over thirty years, yet it seems like they're still in the honeymoon phase.

I want a love like that someday.

I slide the tray into the oven, shut the door, and turn back around at the sound of the back door that leads into the kitchen opening. I can't help but smile at the sight of Hudson walking in with an armful of overflowing grocery bags. My smile drops when I see the look on his face.

He knows.

"Let me help you with those," I rush out, a pain in the back of my throat.

"I've got it," he mutters, setting them on the counter. He kisses Rory on the cheek and then looks over at me. "Can I talk to you for a minute?"

I scrape my hands together and nod. "Sure."

"Don't take too long now," Rory says. "Your father called to tell me people are on their way over. I need all the help I can get."

He tilts his head toward the basement stairs, and I lead the way, gulping with every step.

"What's up?" I ask, turning to look at him.

He pulls his phone out to show me the screen. "Care to explain this?"

I draw in a nervous breath as I read the headline in the photo.

I'm terrified. I'm nervous. I don't want this to be real life.

It's a story about me. About me being a cheater, a liar, everything Hudson hates. It's the same story Willow called me about this morning.

I'm. So. Fucked.

It's worse than I thought.

My hands start shaking. "It …" I pause, scrambling for the right words.

I push myself to fight back the tears. I want to yell that the person in that article isn't me anymore, but I can hear the footsteps upstairs.

People are here.

I take a deep breath. "It happened *one time,* once, with Spencer, and that was before you. It was forever ago. You can't get mad at me for something I did in the past."

He jerks the phone away and slides it back into his pocket in what seems like slow motion.

"I'm not mad that you had sex with him," he replies calmly.

"Yes, you are." I try to match his cool demeanor, but it's difficult.

He's holding himself back. He doesn't want to lose his shit where other people can hear him.

He rubs a palm over his forehead. "You're right. Maybe I am judging you, but it's not because you had a sex life before me. I'm pissed that you had sex with him when you were still with Knox. *You cheated.* You know how I feel about that shit."

I suck my cheeks in. "I … I didn't think it was necessary to tell you about my past screwups."

"You sat there and made me believe you weren't happy with him and that he wasn't a good boyfriend. Not once did you say you weren't a good girlfriend. Not once did you say you cheated on him. Fuck, you even agreed with me that cheaters are terrible people. Meanwhile, you knew you were guilty of the flaw I hate most in people."

I technically never *agreed* with him. Silence isn't agreeing with someone, but I let that go.

"I was lonely and confused," I whisper. "He was never around."

He shakes his head in agony, his eyes cutting down to me. "Jesus Christ, you sound exactly like Cameron."

I wince at his insult. "I'm nothing like her. I would *never* do something like that to you."

"You did it to a man you dated for *years.* A man you were in love with. Why should I think I'd be any different?" He gestures back and forth between the two of us in frustration. "This was all one big mistake."

Tears shimmer in my eyes. "What do you mean?"

"You and me. Why are we wasting our time with something we know isn't going to last?"

I throw my arms up in defeat. "You've barely even given us a chance!"

"Look at the big picture, Stella. We come from two different worlds. Do you plan to move here to be with me? Can you keep your career living here?"

"Well … no."

"Exactly! And your Hollywood life isn't for me! This is my home, where I belong, and California is yours."

"Long-distance relationships can work. I did it with Knox for years."

He scoffs. "News flash, Stella, it didn't work. You cheated, and you guys broke up! That's the worst possible answer you could've given me."

"Fine, I'm a screwup! Is that what you want to hear? That I did something you think so terrible of? It was years ago. I was young, dumb, and lonely."

He runs his hands through his hair in frustration. "You're right, and I understand people make mistakes."

"Thank you." I go to grab his hand, but he recoils at my touch. I should've known it wasn't going to be that easy. "I promise you I will never do anything like that to you. You and me, we're different than how it was with Knox."

"You can't guarantee that," he rasps.

"Yes, I can."

His upper lip curls. "You're doing it to me right now by lying about dating another man. The world thinks I'm screwing you behind his back. We're in a relationship where we can only touch each other behind closed doors. People think you belong to someone else." He grits his teeth. "When you're supposed to be mine. We agreed to go all in, Stella. Now's the fucking time."

"Just give me more time," I plead, my heart racing. "Give me a few weeks."

I promised him that I would end things with Eli, but I can't just do it right now. These things take time. I need to meet with my attorney to look for possible loopholes in the contract and talk to my management company to get them on board. This decision will have consequences.

He flinches. "Does that mean you're going to continue playing pretend with him? You're going to stand there and tell me that you're willing to throw me under the bus and not tell the truth?" He looks at me in disgust. "Unbelievable."

"It's my job, Hudson. What do you expect?"

"What do I expect? Maybe for the girl I'm falling in love with to come clean. To tell them I'm not this terrible man fucking someone else's girl. I expect you not to be ashamed that you're with me."

"Shame? It's not shame. If there's anyone I want to tell the world I'm in love with, it's you!"

Love.

We've both thrown out the word in the past five minutes. You're usually in a good place when you say that to someone for the first time. It ends with kisses, sex, and good feelings.

This is anything but magical. It's a goddamn nightmare. I have no time to relish this moment of him confessing his love because the sadness that he's about to leave me overcomes that.

"Then prove it!" We both flinch at how loud his voice rises, and he controls his breathing before going on, his tone turning soft. "Have Willow put out a statement." He begins to pace in front of me. "This isn't only about us anymore. It'll destroy my family. It'll kill my mother. We're already having a tough time with Lucy's death."

I shut my eyes in embarrassment. I'm selfish. I never even thought about his family. "I'm sorry. I will go up there and tell them the truth about everything."

He stops his pacing and gawks at me. "Just them?"

I look around, unsure of what he's asking me.

"Either you step up and tell everyone the truth, or you need to leave."

His response is like a smack in the face.

"What? You can't … you can't be serious?"

"Two options, Stella. Me or your contract."

"My career is on the line."

"So am I."

I swallow hard. "I can't yet!"

"Then leave. I won't be a man in the shadows." He scrubs his hand over his face, and I notice his eyes are glossy when he pulls it away. "I hate ultimatums and never thought I'd be someone who had to give them to the woman I love, but I have no other choice. You need to make a decision, and there's only one that will keep me."

"*Please*," I whimper. "Give me a few weeks."

He stares at me in disbelief, his eyes cold. "You can stay at Dallas's until Willow finds a bodyguard to fly home with you. Consider this my resignation."

He gives me one last look, one last chance to change my mind, and I do nothing but stare at him with tears in my eyes.

"Have a nice life," he says.

My entire world falls apart at the sight of his back. I stumble to the couch and cry for I don't know how long until I see Lauren tiptoeing downstairs to ask me if I'm ready to go.

I glance around the crowded room for Hudson when I make it upstairs but don't see him. Lauren barely looks at me during the drive to Dallas's and doesn't say a word until she parks in the driveway.

"Look, my brother has been through a lot, and he's a good guy," she says, scowling at me. "If you're not serious about being with him, walk away. Don't hurt someone because you want to have some fun."

I nod and step out of the car at the same time as the tears return.

He begged me for a chance, and I walked away, even after promising him I wouldn't last night. I'm a coward who deserves to be alone, and Hudson deserves someone better than me.

I'm relieved to find Dallas's front door unlocked and the house empty. I left my phone here so it wouldn't go off like wildfire when I was with Rory.

Running downstairs, I start throwing all my shit in my suitcase. I cry as I pick up my phone and notice all the missed calls. I'm going home with a broken heart and a PR nightmare.

When I call for a taxi, I know I'm making the wrong decision.

WILLOW MANAGED to snag me a private flight after we argued back and forth over texts for ten minutes about me traveling without a bodyguard. We fought for another ten minutes after that when I demanded she not tell Hudson about it. I'm no longer his problem.

I don't start opening my texts until I'm on the plane with a glass of wine in my hand.

Eli: What the hell? You said if you did anything, you'd keep it under wraps. I look like a goddamn idiot. Thanks a fucking lot.

Tillie: You need to get back to LA and meet me in my office ASAP.

Willow: Call me please. We need to talk about this. I need to know what you want me to do.

I call Willow. She's been trying to call me for the past hour, but I kept sending her to voicemail. I didn't want to break down in the middle of the airport.

"Jesus, Stella," she blurts out upon answering. "What do you want me to tell all of these people blowing up my phone?"

"Tell them to get fucked," I reply.

"*Whoa,* that's something I've never heard you say, but I'm down with that." She pauses. "What's going on with Hudson?"

I gulp. "He gave me the ultimatum of him or fake dating Eli."

"I'm guessing by the sound of your voice you didn't choose him?"

"I asked for time."

"What if things were reversed? Put yourself in his position. What if you had to sit back and watch him prance around with another woman for months?"

I frown at her valid point. "You're making me feel even more like shit."

"Good. It was my intention. Is your career worth losing him?"

"I told you. My career will never leave me." The tears come back for their next appearance. "You and I both know it'd never work out with him living in BFE and me living in LA."

She sighs. "Looks like we're going to be two bitches going through heartbreak together. I'll pick you up from the airport with new onesies, ice cream, and the sappiest romance movies ever made."

I pull my phone away from my face when it beeps to see the caller. It's what I've been doing since Hudson walked away from me. I get my hopes up, and then they fall when I don't see his name.

He's not calling.

I made that choice and severed everything we built.

"BREAKUPS BLOW DILDOS," Willow says, handing over the tub of ice cream we've been eating from for the past thirty minutes.

"Tell me about it," I mutter with the spoon in my mouth. "So long, good dick; hello, self-induced orgasms. At least the memories stayed with me. I can still imagine Hudson doing it to me every single time. Is that bad? I have a feeling if I saw a therapist, she'd tell me I'm going down the wrong road in my path of trying to get over him."

She slumps down on the couch. "I agree. Men are assholes. Enough said."

I hold up my spoon. "Hear, hear."

She grabs the ice cream from me. "Although I don't feel *that* sorry for you, considering yours is an easy fix. You can have the man you're in love with at the snap of your fingers … or the click of a social media post telling the truth." She shakes her head. "That poor guy is being labeled a bad person when he's actually a pretty chill dude."

I snatch the ice cream back from her and take a bite. "Can it before you're cut off," I say, my mouth full.

It's been twenty-four hours since I landed in LA, and Willow has made it her mission to repeatedly tell me it'd be easy for me to get back with Hudson. I guess she doesn't care about possibly being unemployed because that's what will happen if I do that right now.

"Trust me, misery loves company, but I'd much rather see you happy," she rambles. "And that Muscled Marine makes you happy." She snags the bottle of wine from the coffee table and drinks straight from the bottle. "How was the sex, by the way?"

The wine is the next thing I grab while giving her a dirty look. "I'm in depressed, breakup mode. Do you think I want to talk about Hudson's amazing sex skills?"

"I'll tell you about Brett's."

"Couldn't care less," I sing out.

"Two-pump chump is all I have to say."

I drop my spoon. "You're kidding."

"Nope. The guy couldn't use his fingers to save his life either. Half the time, I thought he had paralysis of the hand when he tried."

"Fuck him and his lame fucking self." I hold up the bottle of wine. "And fuck the men who break our hearts."

CHAPTER THIRTY-FOUR

Hudson

MY LAST PAYCHECK was electronically deposited into my bank account.

I'm drinking away almost every penny of it at Down Home Pub.

I've been the depressed drunk guy sitting in the corner of the bar for the past three hours. People have noticed me but steered clear of approaching. I'm sure I look like a maniac right now. Everyone has been walking on eggshells around me. In pity, I'm sure.

Surprisingly, no one has questioned me about the Stella affair. I'm certain by the stares they give me that they've heard about it. I went to every store in town and bought every magazine with my face on it. The last thing I need is my mom seeing them.

"Fancy seeing you here," Cameron says, pulling out the stool next to me and sitting down.

Perfect.

Just the person I didn't want to see.

"What do you want, Cameron?" I ask, snarling.

"Attitude," she mutters, flipping her hair over her shoulder. "You've changed since you started screwing Little Miss

Superstar. I never pegged you for a guy who went for someone like that. Doesn't seem your type."

I scowl. "I never pegged you for the type to cheat on me with my best friend. I guess we're surprising each other."

Cameron sighs. "I was lonely and confused. Grady was there as a shoulder to cry on. Things escalated. I never meant for it to happen."

I turn to get a good look at her for the first time in a long time. "If you were lonely and confused, you should've talked to me about it. Not jump into bed with someone else, especially my best fucking friend." I swing out my arm, gesturing to the nearly empty bar. "Speaking of Grady, where is your little fiancé? Don't you need a man at your side at all times?"

She blows out a noisy breath. "I'm still in love with you."

"Nice try." I snort and chug the rest of my drink. I'm going to need another if I have to deal with Cameron's shit. She can beg and plead on her knees, but I'll never take her back.

"I tried with Grady. I really did, but I couldn't fight back my feelings for you. He finally couldn't take it any longer. You're embedded inside my soul, Hudson. *You and only you.* I did something terrible, something unforgivable, but I'm begging you to dig into your heart and remember how much you loved me. How happy we were together."

The bartender hands me a whiskey neat, and I take a drink before telling her how ridiculous she sounds.

"How happy we were together?" My voice rises. "You weren't happy, Cameron. You were so damn unhappy that you ran into another man's arms!"

Tears fall down her cheeks. "Please believe it was a mistake. You have to believe me."

"A mistake? So what? You used him until I was ready to give you the life you wanted? Who cares about mine … or even Grady's feelings … just as long as you're getting what you want?"

"It's not like that," she stutters out.

"Yes, it is. You had me, Cameron. You had every single damn piece of me, and you threw it away because you're selfish. Your selfishness cost me my best friend and my trust in love. I will never forgive you for that. I'm sorry, but I can't open myself up to you again. I've realized you're nothing I thought you were. You're not someone I'd ever want to marry."

"But some spoiled television brat is?" she fires back with a sneer. "You know that's not the life you want, and you sure as hell know she's not going to move to Blue Beech and settle down here. Are you going to leave your entire family and move into her mansion while she's making out with other men on TV?" She lets out a childish laugh. "And let's not forget, she cheated on her boyfriend with you. What makes her better than me?"

"You don't know what the fuck you're talking about," I grind out.

"It's all over the internet. You were screwing her behind her little boyfriend's back." She crosses her arms. "What's the difference between her being a cheater and me being one? We did the same thing. Is it different because you weren't the one who got cheated on?"

My stool goes flying backward when I jump up from it. "She was never with him! It was a publicity stunt for their new movie together. They never touched each other behind closed doors. They never shared a bed! *Nothing!* She did all of that with me!" I slam my fist down on the bar. "Me!"

Her tears fall faster as she looks up at me in desperation. "I'm sorry. I didn't know. I thought …"

"Yeah, you spoke before you fucking thought. For someone who's in love with me, you sure don't seem to know me if you'd think I'd do something like that."

"Please," she begs. "Let's go talk somewhere private about this."

I run my hands over my face. "I can't. Sorry. I wish you the best, Cameron, and I hope you find whatever happiness you've been searching for."

CHAPTER THIRTY-FIVE

Stella

"OH FUCK," Willow says, staring at her phone as though she got a notification we're about to be murdered. "Fuckity fuck!"

She and I have spent the week sulking and holding daily *we got our asses dumped* meetings. I won't let her go back to her apartment because I hate being alone.

We go shopping. We do yoga. We try everything to keep our minds off the men we loved and lost.

Some days it works. Some days it doesn't.

The nights are what tears me apart. Thoughts and memories of Hudson haunt me, keeping me up until the morning, and tell me I'm an idiot for not trying to get in touch with him. I haven't even washed my sheets because they smell like him. I'm well aware it's gross.

I haven't called because I'm scared he'll reject me.

He's the one who asked me to leave.

The one who broke things off.

Who didn't want to wait until I could figure out a way to get out of my contract.

But I can't help but feel most of the blame. I was selfish to pursue him when I knew my situation.

"What are you freaking out about over there?" I ask, shoving another bite of ice cream in my mouth while walking on the treadmill.

It's three in the morning, and this is what we're doing.

We're officially losers.

She steps off the bicycle to hold her phone my way and hits the play button. "You're going to want to see this."

A video starts. I trip on my feet, my delicious ice cream falling to the floor, and stare at the screen unblinking when I see Hudson. He's sitting in what looks like a bar arguing with a woman. A woman who looks like Cameron.

"She was never with him!" he screams. "It was a publicity stunt for their new movie together. They never touched each other behind closed doors. They never shared a bed! *Nothing!* She did all of that with me!"

The image is blurry, but there's no doubt it's him. I'll never forget his husky voice. My hand flies to my mouth, and I'm sure that rocky road is about to come up. I jump off the treadmill before I fall and try to control my breathing.

Oh. My. Fucking. God.

Hudson's word vomit just ruined my career in thirty seconds.

"I'm just going to throw this out there," Willow says with a smile. "But I'm pretty sure he's talking about you."

"You think?" I snap.

"I'm also pretty sure the world knows who he's talking about given that it's all over the internet right now." She pulls the phone away, so I can't watch it again. "You're even a trending hashtag."

Fuck me.

I pull my phone from my pocket and open Twitter.

"Seriously?" I yell.

It's #StellaDoesntShareBeds.

"Who comes up with this shit?" I ask.

"It's the internet. A guy banging a McChicken went viral. Your hashtag is lame compared to other ones."

"People have way too much time on their hands."

"Who's the chick in the video?"

"The ex." I hate that she was there with him. That video is going to haunt me for the rest of my life, and I'm going to think about her every time I have to hear about it.

Willow scrunches up her nose. "I wish she were uglier."

"You and me both."

Why was he hanging out in a bar with her?

I know we broke up, and I know I'm still fake dating Eli, but it still hurts.

"He did something you didn't have the balls to do for weeks. Make a public statement and stand up for your relationship."

"He was drunk. If he were sober, it would've never happened."

I slump down on the floor, and she sits down across from me.

"What do I do?" I ask.

My phone starts ringing before I get an answer.

I hold it up to show her the call. "And it gets worse. Tillie is already calling to rip my head off."

"That troll always seems to know everything as soon as it happens. I think she has a tap on our phones. She's like the NSA. Fucking psychopath."

"What do I do?" I repeat.

She perks up and rests her hands in her lap. "First things first. You need to decide if you love the dude or not."

I go silent. I can't seem to form the words to answer her question. They're stuck in my throat as I try to come down from my freak-out. My head is pounding so hard it's making me light-headed.

Am I pissed at Hudson for doing that?

Or more relieved?

I'm not sure.

Willow snaps her fingers in front of my face. "Earth to my

best friend. Are you in love with the dude or only missing his sex organ?"

"Do you think I'd be freaking out this much if I wasn't?"

She scoots in closer to give me a hug.

"I'm scared, Willow."

Her face softens when she pulls away. "Scared to love him?"

I nod.

"Sweetie, don't be afraid to love someone. Love is one of the biggest risks we take because we don't know if it's going to thrive or burn to the ground and take us along with it. But the risk is worth the sting. I promise you that."

I start to fan my face with my hand to fight off the tears. "I know."

She rubs her hands together. "So …"

"I don't want to keep waking up without him."

CHAPTER THIRTY-SIX

Hudson

I WALK INTO MY PARENTS' house with a blasting headache and a hangover from hell. My bright idea of washing my feelings for Stella away with whiskey didn't work out in my favor.

That old pal made me a fucking idiot for the entire world to see. I never wanted to be in the spotlight, never wanted people to know my business, and now I have my phone and email flooded with people offering me money for the inside scoop on Stella's life.

Fucking scavengers.

Dallas sent me the link to the video this morning, and I had to refrain from throwing my phone across the room. My temples throb. I want to put the blame on Stella for this mess. It would've never happened if we didn't start fucking around, but I know the truth. It's unfair for me to blame her for my dumbass getting drunk and opening my big mouth.

"Good morning, idiot," Lauren says when I walk into the kitchen. She narrows her eyes at me in disapproval and slides her plate of half-eaten eggs to the middle of the table. "I saw your obliterated ass on TMZ. Way to keep our family name classy. We were like the Kennedys of Blue Beech, but your behavior has moved us to the lines of the Kardashians. People want to know all of our business, but the respect is gone."

"Don't start your shit," I grumble, making myself a cup of coffee.

I snuck out of Dallas's to avoid his interrogation. Plus, Maven started off her morning living it up with her karaoke machine. Kid's Bop and hangovers don't go well together. And I need to talk to my mom before the mother gang here bombards her on how terrible her son is.

"Oh, I'm just getting started. If you didn't want to hear my mouth, maybe you should've used your pint-sized brain before getting wasted off your ass and bringing attention to our family like this. I swear on everything, if you give Mom a heart attack, I will cut you."

"Chill out. Mom isn't going to have a heart attack. You're overreacting."

She snorts.

"This shit will blow over when the next scandal of a cheating celebrity breaks out. Trust me, I might be popular here, but I'm irrelevant in Hollywood."

"Irrelevant? Is that why we've had several phone calls from reporters? Mom took the phone off the hook and is in the other room reading the Bible so she doesn't have another child breaking people's vows."

"They aren't married. Hell, they aren't even dating."

"Let's add liar to your homewrecker title."

I sit down. "Lauren, I was telling the truth in that video. They were never dating."

"They really were faking a relationship?"

I nod.

"Why the hell would anyone do that?"

"For their career. Publicity. Hype."

She scrunches her face up in disgust. "Sounds like a hooker move to me."

I sigh, remembering the similar conversation I had with Stella about her arrangement.

"You have bad luck in relationships," she goes on. "You might want to change your type or switch teams."

"Says the girl who's also single."

"Hey! My current relationship status is trying to get out of student loan debt and make enough money to survive."

I get up to grab some ibuprofen from the cabinet and fill up a glass of water. "Don't you have a home?"

"Yes, but Mom always makes me breakfast."

"What are you, twelve?" I ask, swallowing down the pills.

"Says the guy crashing in his brother's basement."

I rub the back of my neck to remove some of the tension. Lauren's ass sure as hell isn't helping in the hangover healing. She might be worse than Kid's Bop.

"I have a great idea. How about you eat in silence?" I tell her.

"You've already turned into quite the bossy diva for your short time in Hollywood." She laughs. "You didn't choose the starlet life. The starlet life chose you."

"Enough!" I yell, slamming my glass down, my anger getting the best of me. "Just let it go."

She holds her hands up. "Shit … sorry. I was only trying to make light of the situation."

"I know. I'm sorry." I collapse in the chair next to her again. "I feel like I'm going nuts, and I don't know what to do. I wish I would've never taken that goddamn job."

"Are you in love with her?"

"With Stella?"

She nods.

"No."

"Don't lie to me."

I stay silent.

"I swear I won't give you shit for it."

I snort.

"I want you to find love, especially after what Cameron did to you. If you think this chick is it for you, then I'm all for you fighting for her. But if it's not, if it was only about sex, walk away. Our family can't go through any more stress right now. Only proceed if your feelings are real."

I scrub my hand over my face and groan. "It doesn't matter anymore."

"Why doesn't it matter if you're in love with her?"

"Our lives are complete opposites. All of that being in magazines and people shoving cameras in your face isn't what I want in my life. I want to stay in Blue Beech. She doesn't."

"Have you even asked her if she does, or are you just assuming?"

"It's over. She made her choice. Now, drop it."

"Hudson ..."

I can't handle this conversation right now. I'm growing more nauseated with every second.

"Drop it," I say, my voice stern. "If I don't hear the name Stella again for the rest of my life, I'll be a happy man. I worked for her temporarily. We screwed a few times. It was nothing serious. We were both bored and looking for a good time."

"Keep trying to convince yourself of that, but I know you. You don't do casual sex. You don't screw a girl you don't care about. That's not my brother."

"Maybe it is now."

"YOU LOOK LIKE SHIT," Dallas says when I walk in.

The sucky thing about being close with your siblings is that they're all under the impression they can jump into your business and tell you what to do. It's annoying as fuck even though I know they have my best intentions at heart.

I debated with myself on whether to drink away my sorrows

for the second night in a row, but after what happened last night, it'll be a while before I show my face at the pub again.

"Really?" I ask. "Because I feel fucking fantastic."

He slides a beer across the coffee table to me when I collapse onto the couch. If I can't go to the bar, at least I have him here to bartend and get me hammered.

I hold the bottle out in front of me and take a good look at it. "How come whenever the brain and the heart fight, it's always the liver that suffers?"

"Because it's the easiest one to take our anger out on," Dallas answers, kicking his feet up on the table. "Have you talked to Stella?"

I shake my head.

"She didn't reach out about the video?"

"I wouldn't know even if she did. I turned my phone off to ignore the endless calls. I'm changing my number tomorrow."

"Maybe you should call her."

"She made her choice."

"Did she? Or did you see a stupid magazine headline and push her away because of it? Didn't you give her the ultimatum of you or her career?"

"No, it was *me or Eli.* I'd never force her to give up her career. I only told her I wouldn't be the other man. Don't sit there and act like you wouldn't have done the same thing. Yes, I gave her an ultimatum, which shouldn't be used in relationships, but this situation was different. I'd never force her to do anything she doesn't want to do. She knew they'd rip me apart for that article. She knows how I felt about cheating." I look up at him. "Did you know?"

"About her and Spencer?"

I nod.

"I was there."

I tighten my fingers around the beer bottle.

"Not in the room, but they were at a club, both of them wasted. Stella got into an argument with Knox. She ran into

Spencer, one thing led to another, and he came to our suite with us at the end of the night. Then I went to bed."

"Did he join her in her room?"

"I didn't follow them, but I'm assuming so."

"Why didn't you tell me?"

"It's not my story to tell, and if I recall correctly, you sat in my kitchen saying it wasn't anything serious between you two. If you weren't in a relationship, why does it matter? It was in her past, Hudson. She was young, drunk, and desperate for affection. Her ex was off touring the world and flirting with thousands of women every night. There was a different story about him cheating on her every other day, and she could barely get him on the phone sometimes. Don't hold one mistake over her head. Talk to her. Fix this. You two seemed happy together."

"I could never make her happy."

"Shut the fuck up and quit wallowing in your self-pity."

"I can't give her what those other men can. I don't have access to jets. I can't buy ten-thousand-square-foot homes or extravagant gifts. That's Stella's type, and that will never be me. I was a fuck toy while she couldn't have a real boyfriend."

I'm whining like a little bitch.

His voice lowers. "Stella isn't like that. She won't expect that from you. Do you love her?"

I shrug. "I don't know what I feel anymore."

"Don't bullshit me."

"Would I be this upset if I was trying to bullshit you?"

"Brother, take my word, wasting time on love because of fear is a mistake. You never know how long you have until it's gone. Do it for me. Do it for Lucy. Let love into your heart again before you end up losing it." He wipes tears from his eyes. "All I have to say is I'm encouraging love for everyone around me because I know what it makes you feel. Even in the short time I had with Lucy, it was like a dream come true. My dream life that ended up in a nightmare. I wouldn't change it for anything, though. Time isn't something that's promised to anyone—no matter how rich, how young, or how healthy you are. You can lose everything in the blink of an eye. Don't let it hold you back."

I finish off my beer to give me courage. "I'm having dreams again. They stopped when I was with Stella for some reason, but now they're back."

Dallas sits back to look at me with hooded eyes. "Shit, brother. Why didn't you tell me?"

"It's embarrassing. I'm a twenty-seven-year-old man having nightmares."

"There's nothing embarrassing about PTSD, Hudson. Not one damn thing. You want to talk about it?"

I shake my head. "I'll get through it. Just know I have your back, and I know you've got mine. No matter what bullshit life throws us, we've got this."

CHAPTER THIRTY-SEVEN

Stella

I GRAB my phone from my lap.

"Should I text him?" I stammer out. "I should text him."

I'm in New York for an awards show. Not only is our film nominated in three categories but Eli and I are also up for best couple.

Ha. Best couple.

My stomach has been in knots all day. Per the contract that is ruining my life, I have to walk the red carpet with Eli and act like we're in love. Even with all the shit that went down, the pictures of Hudson and I being leaked, the production company still didn't grow enough balls and put out a statement that we're not an item. We still have to partake in this charade.

Nominated or not, I'm not looking forward to this.

Each day I'm locked into this disaster proves that getting the role wasn't worth it. I turned my back on someone who made me his top priority. No one else has ever done that for me.

And in return, I chose that contract over him.

Joan, my makeup artist, grabs my chin and holds it in place. "What you should do is stay still before he gets a call from a one-eyed chick because she can't stop moving while I finish her eyeliner."

"No, you shouldn't text him," Willow says in a disapproving tone. "You should *call him.* Texting is cowardly in situations like this. Words can be misinterpreted. Texting is for late-night booty calls or telling your asshole ex he was the worst sex of your life. Not for confessing your love and apologizing. Put your big girl panties on. Hit his name. Tell him how you feel before it's too late and he finds some cowgirl out there with honeysuckle straw hanging out of her mouth."

I roll my eyes at her. "How can you sound so smart yet like an asshole at the same time?"

She grins. "It's one of my many talents."

I've been battling with myself on how to fix things with Hudson—if that's even possible.

Is it too late?

I know one thing for sure. I can't live this fake life anymore.

I broke down last night. I missed him. My heart ached to hear his voice. My skin missed his touch. I decided I needed to find a way to make everything right with him. The problem is *how* can I do that?

I sigh, my shoulders slightly slumping, which results in another annoyed look from Joan. "What if he shuts me down? He thinks I'm a cheater, a liar."

"Your behavior and silence make you look like one," Willow argues.

"I want to give you a dirty look right now, but Joan will kick my ass."

"Damn straight," Joan says, adding glue to a false eyelash.

"Call him," Willow demands. "Try. You reaching out will convince him you're not any of those things."

I scoff. "Like it's that easy."

"It really is."

I take a deep breath of courage before hitting his name and then frown at the response. I end the call. "Too late. He changed his number."

"Dickhead," Willow says. "How do you know?"

"That's what the recording just told me," I reply.

Willow points at my phone. "Text Dallas and ask him to give you his new number."

"Isn't that stalkerish?"

"We all stalk people when we're in love."

Joan takes a break from me to look over at Willow. "Pretty sure stalking is illegal whether you're in love with the person or not."

I nod in agreement. "We need to find you a boyfriend stat before you end up in the looney bin."

"Says the girl who doesn't have one either."

I open my mouth for my next smart-ass comment but stop when I hear the sound of the suite's front door slamming shut.

"Fuck that shit!" an irate voice yells.

Eli comes storming into the room with Tillie on his heels, fury blazing off the both of them. His manager, a quiet guy I've never even had a conversation with, walks in a few seconds later, worry clear on his face.

"Eli," Tillie says cautiously.

He points at me with a snarl. "I'm not walking the red carpet with her. I refuse to look like a desperate man okay with his girlfriend fucking around on him. This dating deal is over. I played my part. Paid my dues. You want someone to sue, sue her ass. She's the one who got busted fucking another dude."

I can't blame Eli for his animosity. I would've reacted the same way if photos leaked of him with another girl. No one wants to look like the idiot who stayed with the cheater.

"What if I release a statement denying her affair with the bodyguard?" his manager asks. "They're friends. That's it. The picture was taken at a weird angle."

Willow snorts.

Joan laughs.

"People aren't fucking dumb," Eli snarls. "Any angle will show them sucking each other's faces off and fucking."

"Why do you even care?" I ask. "You got what you wanted. You can go out and have your fun now."

"No, I fucking can't." He tilts his head toward Tillie. "*This bitch …*"

My mouth, along with everyone else's except for Tillie's, falls open. Eli is as over it as I am. Thankfully, he's doing the talking for me. Tillie doesn't seem fazed at his name-calling. I'm sure it's not the first time she's been called that and worse.

"She's threatening to sue me if we don't continue this lie," Eli goes on. "Not happening. I will jump my ass on stage and tell everyone the truth."

"And risk your reputation?" Tillie asks.

"New plan. We'll tell them you decided to go your separate ways," Eli's manager says. "No one needs to know about the agreement."

"How about we don't go?" I suggest.

"Not happening," Tillie says. "Nice try, though."

I'm still on her shit list and also positive she wants to suffocate me in my sleep.

"See what you caused because you had to go screw around with the bodyguard, for God's sake," Tillie says to me before leaving the room.

I flip her the bird.

"That chick needs some dick herself," Joan comments. "She's in one hell of a bad mood." She brings her attention back to me. "You better not ruin this face I spent thirty minutes working on with tears."

I look up in the mirror and realize I'm crying. "Shit," I say, wiping away tears.

"I hope you're not shedding tears over that bitch," Joan goes on. "She isn't shit. Don't let her control your life. If you like a guy, be with him. Why is that such a problem?"

Willow hands me a tissue. "That's what I've been saying. What are you going to do?"

Tillie being mad isn't why I'm upset. These are tears of

regret for letting other people control my life and causing me to lose someone I love.

"I hope it's to stop fucking crying," Joan says. "Think about something happy before you ruin my artwork over here. It's disrespectful."

I roll my eyes. "Happiness isn't something I'm capable of right now."

"How can we help?" Willow asks.

"Bring him back to me," I answer."

She throws a makeup brush at me. "Then what the hell are you doing, Stella? I can't fix that. Joan can't fix that. *You* have to do something. You have to go to him."

"I have responsibilities here that I can't walk away from," I argue.

"Uh … yes, you can."

"Don't be funny," I mutter.

"I'm being honest. You have no obligations right now. You aren't working on a project. You have nothing holding you back. *Nothing.* You have enough money that you could retire tomorrow if you wanted to. Take time off. Find yourself."

"I'm still obligated to go to this stupid ass award show."

"What if I tell them you got food poisoning and puked all over your dress?" She jumps up from her chair as if it's the best idea she's ever had. "You can't show up naked."

I shake my head. "That's not happening. I'll go to the awards show and figure out what to do with my life when it's over."

CHAPTER THIRTY-EIGHT

Hudson

I PEEK up from furniture shopping on my laptop when I see Dallas walk into his guest bedroom. I'm still crashing here until I move into the house I signed a lease for yesterday. Starting over will be a bitch, but I won't be asking Cameron for my furniture back.

I shudder, thinking about the fact she brought another man into our bed.

Thank fuck I dodged that bullet.

"You. Me. Guys' night in," he declares. "We've been some depressing ass dudes on the brink of singing Taylor Swift songs if we don't get our shit together. Lauren kidnapped Maven for the night, so we can drink all the alcohol we want."

"What's wrong with Taylor Swift?" I question. "'Shake It Off' is a good jam. Maven is making me a fan."

He laughs, shaking his head. "Oh hell, he's growing a heart again."

I flip him off. "Guys night sounds good to me."

I'm up for anything that'll keep my thoughts off Stella. I've been trying to *shake her off* by staying busy, but it's not working. It's worse at night. I stay up thinking about her, and then when I finally do doze off, I'm woken up by another flashback.

Shit sucks.

Even though our time was limited, there's something about her I can't let go.

We were both lost and fell right into each other's laps at the time we needed somebody the most.

Love can build up over time, or it can tear into you like a storm—sweeping you off your feet—and you have no idea what happened. You have no time to prepare yourself for surviving or for the devastation of heartache. That's what I experienced with Stella. I fell for her and crashed into her waves before I realized I even stepped outside.

I never believed in instant love until her.

I never thought I'd crave someone I'd only known a month until her.

I was brought up with the notion that love assembles with time. That's what happened with Cameron, with my parents, with everyone I know. But that wasn't the case with Stella. Love can assemble with conversations, with sweet gestures, with making the other person feel as though they're perfect in your eyes.

And fuck do I miss her … miss that rush.

And the world isn't helping me move on.

She's everywhere.

Every-fucking-where.

In real life.

In my dreams.

Even Maven is finding it crucial to watch reruns of her show that are now streaming on Netflix.

New rule: no dating anyone who's on TV.

I WALK into the living room with a beer in each hand and plop down on the couch before handing one to Dallas.

I'm making myself comfortable when he changes the channel.

"What the hell, dude?" I snap. I'm not pissed that he changed our regular programming of sports. It's what he turned it to. "Guys' night involves drinking and staying the fuck out of our feelings. Next channel please."

Seeing her will tear me apart, and I sure as fuck won't put myself through hell if I don't have to.

He looks at me from the other side of the sectional while trying his best to look innocent. "What are you talking about? I've been waiting for this all week."

I throw my arm out toward the TV and narrow my eyes. "You've been counting down the days to watch *The Teen Choice Awards*?"

He nods.

"Something you've never taken an interest in before. Not even when we were teens."

"It looked good. Maven asked me to watch to tell her everything when she gets home tomorrow."

"Fucking liar. What it looks like is you setting me up."

He grins. "You have two options. *The Little Mermaid* or this."

"The fuck? Last time I checked, you had every single damn channel known to man."

"True, but I'm hosting guys' night, which means I get to choose what we watch."

I settle back in my seat. "Screw it. Whatever your plan is, it's not going to work."

He holds up his hands. "No plan here."

I stop myself from calling him out on his shit. He's having fun with this, something he hasn't had in a long ass time.

Might as well give him what he wants.

CHAPTER THIRTY-NINE

Stella

MY HEART IS close to bolting out of my chest.

I've never done anything like this before.

This decision could obliterate my career even more than it has since the whole Eli-Cheat-Gate. It's not like it's at its highest point right now anyway.

Eli's shoulder bumps into mine when he leans in from his seat to bitterly whisper in my ear. "We better not win this shit. You can bet my ass I won't go up there and accept that award with you."

Tillie eventually convinced—well, threatened—Eli to come. He drew the line at walking the red carpet or participating in any interviews, and surprisingly, she agreed. And even more shockingly, she allowed me to do the same, which most likely only happened because she didn't want me to be interrogated.

News has been slow these past few weeks, so our so-called cheating scandal has been a shitstorm with Eli being the brunt of the jokes. Humiliation is destructive to a career in this industry. Tabloids and the internet will never let you live it down.

We're in the front row of the awards show that's thirty minutes in. Thirty minutes too long. I can't wait to get out of here. I run my hand down my dress when the presenter starts naming the nominees in our category. Winning the award isn't what's important to me.

It's the opportunity I want.

The moment.

I lose my chance if we lose.

Unless I pull a Kanye.

The presenter, a girl I've worked with on my show before, opens the envelope and squeals before screaming our names for best movie couple.

"You've got to be fucking kidding me," Eli mutters, covering his face to hide his aggravation from the cameras.

He stands up, which goes against what he said he'd do, but doesn't bother helping me out of my chair. His manners do come through when he waits for me before going on stage. He helps me up the stairs, so I don't bust my ass in my eight-inch heels.

The crowd is clapping.

Fan girls who post Instagram photos of us with #relationshipgoals are squealing in excitement.

Relationship goals.

Ha. We're nothing but phonies.

Eli stands back, his arms crossed, and gestures for me to go ahead. All eyes are on me when I stand in front of the microphone. My stomach knots so tight it physically hurts, but I have to do this. I close my eyes and take a calming breath before I let my confession slip through my lips.

"I want to start by thanking our fans who watched the movie and voted for us," I begin. "You have given me so much in my career—showed me compassion and honesty. I've let you down by not giving that honesty back."

Eli's chest hits my back as his lips go to my ear. "Don't fucking do it, Stella," he hisses, grabbing my elbow.

I jerk myself from his hold and continue. "For as long as I can remember, there's been speculation about my life. I grew up in the public eye—everyone witnessing the best and worst times of my life—whether I liked it or not. The negative stories, they hurt, and I faked who I was to prevent them. Acceptance is all I wanted in this merciless industry. I put other people's approval before my happiness and believed my happiness and that approval was dependent on what I was wearing … who my friends were … who I was dating." I start to choke up but force myself to push through, even when the tears start. "I wasn't following my heart." My hand presses to my chest. "I'd like to apologize for not doing that, for being dishonest to myself and you. I never cheated on Eli. We were never a couple."

Eli is walking off the stage when I glance back to silently apologize.

I inhale another breath before continuing. I've already started digging my grave—might as well jump in. "I can't continue choosing my career, my reputation, over my happiness. You'll never get the best of me if I do. I was hurting myself and the man I love to make everyone else happy. I can't do that anymore."

Jaws are dropping, and phones are up, recording me, no doubt. My vision grows blurry from my tears.

I've never felt so free.

I swipe a fresh tear from my face as applause erupts around the room.

I whip around in my heels, and the cameras follow me as I flee backstage, where Willow is waiting.

"I am so fucking proud of you," she squeals. "Now, we have to get you out of here before the rest of the mob shows up. I have a car waiting for us."

"Thank you," I breathe out.

My new bodyguard follows me through the hallway while I keep my head down and ignore the camera flashes and questions about my relationship with Hudson. A rush of cold air and relief hits me when we walk out the exit doors.

Willow shoves my phone in my hand as soon as we slide into the back seat of the SUV with tinted windows.

I immediately text Dallas.

Me: Did you get him to watch it?

I fan myself with my hand. My heart is in the grips of a man I'm not sure even wants anything to do with me.

I took the risk.

I hope he does the same.

"Calm down before you have a heart attack," Willow orders. "Dallas has your back and wants his brother to be happy. Let's hope he hog-tied him, or whatever those country people do, to a chair and made him watch."

"Even if he did, that doesn't mean it'll change Hudson's mind about me."

I almost drop my phone when it vibrates.

Dallas: I did. His reaction wasn't pretty. I'm sorry, Stella.

No. No!

Why did I wait so long?

Why did I hold back on something that made me feel whole?

Hudson isn't one for grand gestures. He's simple. All he asked for was honesty and commitment. He gave me so many chances to give it to him, but I was too stubborn. I walked away and tore down everything we built.

My hands are shaking as I type out my response.

Me: It's fine. Thank you for trying.

"Tell me it's good news," Willow says.

I can tell she already knows from the crestfallen look on her face.

"It's over," is all I can whimper. My hands are still shaking. My legs are shaking. I'm shattering everywhere. "I need to accept that."

She scoots in closer to pull me in for a hug. "He'll come around."

I shake my head. "No. He's too headstrong. You should've

seen his face when I chose to leave. It was a mixture of disgust and regret. He lost all feelings for me when I told him I wasn't going to tell the truth."

I start to scrape away at my fresh manicure in an attempt to calm myself. She squeezes me one last time and pulls away when her phone goes off. Her eyes grow wide as she reads a text and then frantically starts smashing her fingers against the screen.

"Who are you talking to?" I ask. "In case you forgot, I'm over here having a crisis."

"You're having a pity-party before you've even given him time," she argues, still concentrating on her phone.

"Fine." I cross my arms and pout. "Tell me who you're talking to."

"Damn, nosy." She rolls her eyes. "It's Brett's cheating ass. He wants to get back together."

"Vomit. Please tell me you're not considering it?"

"Hell no." She's still typing like she's writing a farewell letter before dying.

"Stop entertaining him then."

She laughs. "I enjoy watching him squirm."

"Like he squirmed his pint-size wiener into vaginas that weren't yours?"

"Pretty much."

"How about I help you out with that and stop you from doing something stupid." I attempt to snatch her phone, but she's faster than I am.

"Nice try. Let me have my fun. Don't blame a girl for enjoying breakup revenge. They seem to always come back sniffing around when they realize you're done playing their games and have moved on."

"If only Hudson were a douchebag like Brett."

She darkens her screen and slips her phone into her bag. "If that were the case, you wouldn't be sacrificing your career for him. That was a big step, and I'm proud of you."

"Glad I have your support for being unemployed and single

the rest of my life." I moan out in irritation. "I need carbs. I need alcohol. I need carbs mixed with alcohol."

I TURNED my phone off after reading the text from Dallas, handed it to Willow, and made her promise not to give it back under no circumstances until tomorrow—even if I threatened to cut her hair off while she's sleeping.

I'm avoiding all forms of communication in fear of what people are saying about my speech.

"When I declared I was going off the grid, I assumed you'd do the same," I whine.

We're back in the hotel and lounging in bed wearing our pajamas. It's been three hours since I humiliated myself in front of millions of people. It's felt like three hundred days. Willow has been on her phone nonstop since we got back to the room and refuses to let me read the texts from Brett.

She looks over at me, raising a brow, while sitting cross-legged across from me. "You know what they say when you assume."

I roll my eyes. "Whatever. You officially suck at being a heartbroken wing-woman."

Her face turns serious. "I'm your assistant. I have to make sure people aren't talking too much shit about you. My mother is also texting me about your drama. I swear, that woman is more interested in your relationships than my own." She holds her phone out to me. "If you're so bent out of shape about it, you can text them back."

I wave my hand through the air when her phone beeps again. "Forget it. Go right ahead. Make that thing useful and order some food while you're at it. I'd like alcohol and ice cream to be our guests of honor."

"Don't you think you have enough here?" She jerks her head toward the bottle of vodka sitting on the nightstand.

I opened it about an hour ago after throwing my shoes across the room and declaring I was swearing off men for the rest of my life. What's better than being a heartbroken hot mess? Being a *drunken* and heartbroken hot mess.

I jump up on my knees. "Oh my god! Speaking of ice cream, don't they make some with alcohol in it now?" *That's my kind of dessert.* "If you find it and get it delivered, I'll give you a raise."

"If I do, you'll stop bitching about me being on the phone?"

"Stay on your phone all you want, and I'll enjoy my alcohol and sugar."

"Challenge accepted."

"ARE YOU DEAD?" I stutter to Willow's voicemail. I searched the place for my phone and found it hidden in a bathroom cabinet. "It's been twenty-five minutes since you said you were meeting the delivery guy in the lobby. Where did you find it? Craigslist?" I slap my hand against my mouth and hiccup. "I'm a terrible person. I got my best friend murdered over ice cream desperation."

I continue to ramble how I'll make sure she has a good funeral but stop when I hear the door open. I end the call, and the phone bounces on the mattress when I drop it. I slide off the bed and nearly face plant in the process of rushing into the living room.

"Fuck, Willow, why aren't you answering your phone? I thought I was going to have to identify your body," I screech. I'm throwing my arms in the air and dramatically stomping my feet.

I skid to a sudden stop.

My breathing restricts like all the air has been sucked out of the room.

Hudson stands only a few feet away from me in a wide

stance. His hands are pushed into the front pockets of his ripped jeans, and his whiskey-colored eyes stare into mine with uncertainty. I rub my eyes—certain the alcohol is toying with my mind.

"Your new bodyguard needs fired," is his icebreaker.

I relax at the sound of his gentle voice. He's not angry or here to yell at me for wronging him. He's here to be the Hudson I fell in love with—the rough on the outside man who opened up his softer side to me.

"It's hard finding someone as skilled as you," I whisper, stumbling over my words.

What does this mean?

Is he here to ask me not to talk about him in public … or did my speech change something?

I run my hands through my tangled hair. It's not how I'd planned on seeing him in our moment of reconciliation, but it's how he prefers me, so no need to stress about it. He appreciates the real me, not my money, my fame, or how I look after an hour with my glam squad.

I don't move when he takes a step closer.

"I had a guys' night tonight," he tells me.

I look around in confusion. "Okay?"

"We ended up watching some awards show."

I cover my face in humiliation. "Please tell me you turned the channel before they announced best couple?"

He grins wildly. "But that was my favorite part, Hollywood."

I move my hand to reveal a timid smile. "So, it worked?"

He takes another step. We're only arm's length away from each other. "It brought me here."

"Is that a yes?"

He takes that last stride, stopping in front of me, and grabs my hand. I stagger a bit when he leads me over to the sofa and sits us down so we're facing each other.

"I know you're probably pissed at me, and you have every right to be," he says.

I flinch. *Me pissed at him*?

I was the one who chose my career over us.

"It was killing me to watch you pretend to be with another man. *Fucking killing me,*" he stresses, his face turning grim. "Even though it was one of the hardest decisions I've ever had to make, there was no choice for me but to let you go."

I clutch at my chest. "But I was yours. I told you that. I wanted nothing more than to be yours! I didn't want Eli. I wanted you!" My eyes start watering, and I can feel the tears ready to unveil.

"Actions speak louder than words, and your actions were playing the fake girlfriend of another man. I couldn't even touch the woman I loved in public. When those pictures of us leaked, even though I never wanted it to happen, I thought that maybe it was a good thing—maybe you'd be honest and choose us. But you didn't. Instead, you fled and left me hanging out to rot like the bad guy treading on some other dude's woman, when, in actuality, it was my heart getting stomped on."

"I know, and I'm so sorry! I had too many people wanting too many things from me." My buzz is beginning to wear off.

"All I wanted from you was to choose me. You can have your career. You can have the life you want. I want you to be happy and to be part of what's making you happy. I wanted to hear you say those words, Stella! I wanted to hear, *to feel,* that you were falling in love with me as much as I was you."

Whoa. My heart starts racing.

"I do fucking love you!" I tell him. "I realized I couldn't lose you, and in case you missed it, I did in front of millions of people. If you don't believe what I said was true, turn on the TV, log onto the internet, and watch it again. You can hear you're the only one I want."

"I saw it. It's not that I don't believe you. What I'm trying to say is that even though I appreciate the gesture, that's not what I needed."

"What do you need then?"

"For you to choose me and not make me share." He shakes his head. "Maybe I should've given you more time. I don't know where we went wrong or what could've changed the outcome. All I know is I'm here to say I'm sorry."

I take his hand in mine. "I'm sorry for everything. I've been doing some soul-searching."

He chuckles. "With the help of alcohol, I see."

I narrow my eyes his way. "Hey! I'm not perfect."

He squeezes my hand and brushes his thumb along the edge. "I'm not expecting you to be. I mean, technically, you're perfect in my eyes. But in reality and relationships, perfection is unrealistic. All I'm asking from you is honesty and loyalty. I can deal with any other bullshit thrown our way. I promise to give you the same." His other hand reaches out, and he uses his thumb to wipe my tears away. "And I sure as fuck don't want to make you cry."

I point at my face. "Tears of joy. I promise."

He brushes a tangled strand of hair away from my face. "And drunkenness, which is why I think we need to stop any other serious conversations for tonight. I want you sober when we figure things out."

I perk up. "You're going to stay?"

"I'm not going anywhere."

I grin.

He grins.

I'm drunk and lovestruck. Nothing else matters at this moment but the two of us. Not what other people think. Not the consequences of my speech.

Nothing.

He pulls me closer, and I turn, making myself comfortable with my back against his hard chest, and relax.

He feathers his fingers down my arm. "You want to know one of the biggest things I've missed about us?"

"The blowjobs?"

He chuckles. "Yes, I've definitely missed those, but what I

miss the most is sharing a bed with you. I loved waking up next to you in the morning. I don't know how, but you shine a light on my flashbacks and nightmares. I don't feel anything but happiness when you're in my arms."

I tilt my head back, and he moves in to press his lips against mine. Our mouths linger before we separate. I've missed this so much. Nothing compares to being in his arms.

"I feel nothing but happiness when I'm there. You make me feel like I'm enough, like no matter what mistakes or decisions I make, I won't lose you," I tell him before something hits me, and sweep my eyes over the room. "Uh, have you seen Willow?"

"She and Dallas are grabbing a bite to eat," he answers. "I booked her a room so we could talk."

Thank God.

I raise my brow. "Talk, eh?"

"Trust me, there will be much more than talking in the morning. I'll be giving you speeches with my tongue between your legs as breakfast."

I shiver. "I have something to look forward to. Hopefully, it cures hangovers."

He chuckles. "If not, we can try other ways."

"I like the sound of that, and before I forget to ask, you said Willow *and Dallas* are grabbing a bite to eat. He's here?"

"He decided to come with me. It'll be good for him to get out of town. I know people mean well, but they're still dropping off condolence pies and flowers. It's tearing him apart."

"I agree. Willow is probably giving him a tour and forcing him to visit every food truck. She loves this city. I take it this was planned, and everyone was in on it but me?"

"After I saw your speech, I texted Willow telling her I needed to see you. I asked her not to ruin the surprise."

Hell, this was a setup. She wasn't texting douchebag Brett. Her sneaky ass was texting Hudson. I can't believe she didn't hide the alcohol if she knew he was coming. I'm sure it would've looked very suspect had she taken the liquor. Her sneakiness has made me goddamn happy, so I guess she'll get a raise and a new puppy or something.

"TILLIE, Tillie, Tillie, my mom, my sister." I'm reading off the list of voicemails on my phone.

It's morning, but the sun isn't blessing me with its presence thanks to the thick curtains. My brain is playing ping-pong with my skull.

"Reporter," I continue. "TMZ. Reporter. Buzzfeed. Tillie. My manager." I sigh, tossing my phone on the floor. "It might be time to change my number."

"Or block Tillie," Hudson says, lifting himself up with his elbow and resting his chin in his palm, smiling down at me.

I love waking up next to him. His hair is a tousled mess, and his gaze on me is gentle. Tilting his head forward, he brushes his lips along the tip of my nose.

"That crazy ass woman is most likely searching the streets for you and punching people in the face when they tell her they have no idea where you are," he adds. "We need to come up with a plan on how to handle her."

Kill her?

"Willow emailed my attorney in case she tries to sue me and take my firstborn."

My perfect assistant not only has my back personally but professionally as well. She jumped with glee when I told her my speech idea. She pulled out her phone and immediately began drafting an email to my attorney and publicist, waiting to hit send until it actually happened. Willow might be little, but the chick gets shit done.

"Don't you mean our firstborn?" he corrects.

That sentence shoots a spark right through my veins, waking my ass up. Bring on the sunshine. I suddenly feel rejuvenated, at the top of the world, and am on the verge of getting up to perform a happy dance. I no longer think I'd be a bad mom with Hudson at my side. I'll be fine, and there's not a doubt in my mind he will be an amazing father. He's great with Maven.

I can already imagine it.

I stare up at him, our gazes meeting, and I can feel my smile growing. "Let me correct myself. *Our* firstborn."

"Just wanted to clarify," he says, his grin matching mine. I shudder when his fingers dance over my arm. "Now that we've had the children talk, how about we rewind and have the pre-baby talk?"

He stayed true to his word last night. We didn't have a big relationship conversation. He made me drink plenty of water, told me to make myself comfortable in his arms on the couch, and we watched TV until I dozed off. He then carried me to bed and tucked me in.

Yesterday started out in hell and ended up in heaven.

Heaven is about to cloud when we bring up plans, compromises … and the miles that separate us.

Why can't we skip the serious relationship questions?

Love … that's why.

It always seems to make everything so damn complicated.

He laughs when I groan. "We held off until you were sober, so where should we start?"

I sit up. "I can change that. I didn't get a chance to finish the vodka last night."

He stops me from sliding out of bed. "Nice try."

I frown, and his tone turns serious. Not stern-like, but more like a straight to business voice. "What's the next step?"

"I want to take some time off," I answer, timidly looking at him. "I thought I could maybe stay in Iowa with you?"

My idea catches him off guard, and his response does the same to me.

"You don't have to do that."

"What do you mean?"

"I don't want you to change and completely uproot your life

for me. You love acting. It's in your heart. I can't ask you to give it all up and move to Blue Beech. You wouldn't be happy."

I hold my hand out to stop him. "I'm not saying I want to retire or start raising cattle. I've been thinking about taking a break for a while now because I haven't found a role I've liked. I'll have my manager keep an eye out for anything that might catch my interest." I snuggle in closer to him. "Meanwhile, I'd like to get out of the spotlight until everything dies down."

"You promise? I don't want you to make this decision because you think it's what I want. We can work something out. California isn't my ideal home, but I would move there if it meant being with you. Hell, I'd be happy anywhere if you're by my side."

"Me too, which is why I want us to try Iowa out. Just for a while … a test run."

He leans down and nudges my nose with his. "Privacy does sound pretty damn good."

I grin against his lips. "Doesn't it?"

"Just promise me one thing."

"What's that?"

"If you don't like it, you'll tell me."

"I promise." I scoot in closer, tangling my legs with his. "Now, I believe you also made some promises last night. Something about helping me with my hangover. How about you let me clear my head by giving me some?" I shiver when his hand sweeps down my thigh and slides between my legs.

"How about I make you orgasm that hangover out of you and then let you suck my cock until you feel hydrated?"

"Sounds like the perfect remedy."

CHAPTER FORTY

Stella

Six Months Later

"I HAVE A SURPRISE FOR YOU," I sing out, swinging my hips in the kitchen while making a cup of coffee.

I shiver when Hudson comes up behind me to sweep his arms around my hips and brushes his soft lips along my neck.

"Oh, really?" He chuckles in my ear. "How about you give me a clue?"

I twist in his hold and circle my arms around his neck before kissing him. "Nuh-uh, that would ruin everything I have planned."

He plants his lips back against mine, taking the opportunity to slide his tongue inside my mouth. He tastes like fresh mint. "I'll work for it."

"Gross! Chill out, tonsil scrubbers," Willow says.

I glance over Hudson's shoulder to find her pulling out a chair at the kitchen table and sitting down.

"Be considerate of those who aren't exactly love's biggest fans at the moment." She narrows her green eyes and gestures back and forth between Hudson and me. "This kind of cheesy behavior will not only ruin my breakfast, but it will also wreck your argument of convincing me to move to this godforsaken town that consists of a total of five square miles."

Her mouth drops open when I start slicing my finger across my neck in warning repeatedly until Hudson looks down at me in confusion. I straighten my stance and shrug, trying my best to appear clueless.

He pulls away. "You're considering moving here … permanently?"

I can see the excitement dancing in his eyes.

I'm also giving Willow the dirtiest look I can manage.

"Not *permanently,*" she rushes out, answering for me while trying to save both of our asses. "Don't get your balls all up in a bunch, country boy. That came out all wrong. *What I meant* is that she's trying to get me to stay here *when she is.*"

I love California. It's been the place I called home since I was in diapers, but these six months I've spent in Blue Beech have been a breath of fresh air. I've never felt so free.

After the awards show and Hudson's surprise visit, we spent the next two days in New York before flying to Iowa. The first few weeks were hectic. The paparazzi continued stalking me, but they eventually gave up when they figured out I wasn't giving them anything regarding Eli-Cheat-Gate. They moved on to search for the next celebrity scandal.

Willow went back to LA, packed some of my things, and mailed them to Hudson's rental. She's been staying in California since I haven't needed her for anything, but I will now, so persuading her to make this her new home is my goal while she's visiting this weekend. She's not into the idea yet, but I'm going to make her fall in love with Blue Beech like I did.

Hudson chuckles and kisses me on the cheek before grabbing his travel mug. "Don't keep me clueless for too long." He winks and signals back and forth between Willow and me.

"I'm headed to work. You two maniacs stay out of trouble and let me know if you need anything."

He and Dallas are working for their dad's company and trying to expand the business. They've been attending auctions to buy farm equipment, then fixing them up to sell to local farmers.

Willow salutes him. "Aye aye, captain."

He gives me another cheek kiss and leaves while a cheesy smile spreads across my face.

"Have I told you how much I like that dude?" Willow asks. "Who would've thought once you pulled that stick out of his ass, he would be hilarious and fun?"

"It's the environment," I say, grinning wildly. "Everything is more exciting in Blue Beech."

Her eyes sharpen my way. "Don't even try it. I told you I'd give you this weekend for your whole surprise party thing, and then I'm back to the city where I can get takeout sushi on every corner."

"I CAN'T BELIEVE you pulled this off without me finding out," Hudson says as he looks around Magnolia's.

The bakery is packed with a mixture of people from Blue Beech and out-of-towners. It was the perfect place for me to throw a party. I haven't seen some of these people in nearly a year, and I'm sure most of them are going to break my kneecaps when they realize they'll be surrounded by baked goods all night.

Carbs. Sugar. Butter.

All of the things I'd once tried my best to steer clear of are now something I treat myself to at least once a week.

"It's been hard," I reply. "But so worth it."

"You ready to spill the beans?"

I jump up and down in excitement. "Let me introduce you

to someone first." I snag his hand and lead him over to an older man wearing a polo and dark jeans.

"This is Max," I introduce. "He was the executive producer for my old show."

Hudson shakes his hand. "It's nice to meet you."

I take a deep breath. *Here goes.* "I didn't say anything, in case I was getting my hopes up, but I pitched an idea to him about filming a show here in Blue Beech a few months ago."

"You're shitting me?" Hudson bursts out. He points at Max when I shake my head. "And you … you bought it?"

"Sure did," Max replies.

I jump again, adding a squeal this time. It's been hell holding on to this information for the past month. When something good happens, the first person you want to share it with is the one you love.

"They not only bought it. They *love it,*" I yell. "I'll be playing an actress who moves to a small town when her career fails after a publicity crisis."

He runs his hands through his hair, every trace of excitement vanishing from his face. "Jesus, let's hope it's not based on a true story."

Max chuckles. "I can promise you it's not." He tilts his head my way. "I've known Stella for years. Talent like hers can never fail."

Max then goes into the details. We've already found the perfect location thirty minutes out of town to film at and plan to start shooting in three months. I've never been so thrilled about a project.

"You don't feel that way, do you?" Hudson asks when Max leaves to talk to one of the writers. "That you're becoming a failed actress? I don't want you to stay here if it's not what you want. I know you love to act, and I don't want to hold you back from that."

"Absolutely not," I affirm. "It's *loosely* based on my life with the experiences of this change. I'll learn that there's more to love in a small town than I imagined. I never thought I'd feel this way about a place like this and the people here. My dream is to act and be happy. I'll have both of them here." I take his hand and squeeze it. "I swear to you. This is what I want."

It's the truth. Once word got out that I wasn't having an affair with Hudson, Blue Beech greeted me with open arms. They see me as *me* now. Not the celebrity. They don't snap pictures when I'm shoving a cupcake down my throat, or when Hudson slips me a kiss in the town circle after a parade. There hasn't been a photo of us leaked in four months.

He steps in closer, lowering his voice. "We're going to do this, huh? Settle here and make a life?"

I grin. "Damn straight, we are."

He clasps his hands on my cheeks and brushes his lips against mine. "I'm not sure what I did to deserve someone who keeps making me the luckiest man alive. I love you."

"I love you."

"WHERE ARE WE GOING?" I ask when I notice Hudson doesn't turn down our street on the way home from Magnolia's.

We came. We conquered cupcakes. Then the bakery slowly started to clear out as people left to crash into their sugar-induced comas.

Hudson looks over at me, his hands on the steering wheel. "You thought you were the only one who could keep a surprise?"

"Sneaky ass," I mutter. I rub the back of my neck while trying to think of what his surprise could be.

Holy shit, is he going to propose?

I play with my hands in my lap as my nerves go batshit crazy. Surprises aren't as fun when you're not the one keeping them.

I crank my head to the right when he turns down his

parents' street and up a dirt drive. He jumps out of the cab and circles the truck to open my door. He grabs my hand, snags a flashlight from the bed, and walks us into the middle of the field.

I take a look around. "I'm a little confused here."

He chuckles. "I've been talking to my parents. They have so much land here, more than they know what to do with, so I offered to take some off their hands." He drops my hand and turns in a circle. "What do you think about building Casa Barnes-Mendes here?"

I'm staring at him, bug-eyed and silent.

He scratches his cheek. "If it's not something you want, tell me. It's not set in stone yet."

I jump up into his arms and wrap my legs around his waist. He holds me up as I stare down at him with a smile.

"Yes!" I yell. "Yes!"

"You had me terrified for a second."

I brush my lips against his. "I enjoy watching you squirm." I run my hands down his chest as I slide back to my feet. "This is the perfect plan."

"Now, how about I take you to our temporary home and show you how much that excites me?"

"I like the way you think, but first, we need to find Willow."

"Ah yes, Lauren texted me and said she took Willow under her wing tonight. The Down Home Pub is having a live band play, and when I told Lauren about your new show, she decided to sign up for the Operation Get Willow to Move Here Team. She's going to drop Willow off later tonight. They thought we needed some solo-celebrating time."

"I love friends who care about their friend's sex lives. Let's get home before our company gets back."

CHAPTER FORTY-ONE

Stella

I CAN DECLARE last night as being one of the best of my life.

I want to replay it over and over again.

Hudson's eyes flutter open when I lift myself to straddle his waist in bed. I shiver, the chilly air hitting my back after leaving the heat of our sheets, but I have a feeling he'll warm me up.

His promise to show his excitement for all the progressive steps we took last night continued well into the morning. The scent of sex wavers through the room, reminding me of all the dirty things we did to each other last night. I'm running on only a few hours of sleep, but I'll never be too exhausted for him.

A low groan escapes his throat when he clasps his hands onto my waist, his fingers biting into my bare hips. "Damn baby, good morning to you, too," he growls out, rocking his hips up so I can see just how *good* my surprise is.

I moan at the friction of his erection rubbing in *almost* the right spot. His hand climbs forward to cup my breast, and I throw my head back when he uses a single finger to tease my nipple.

I'm wide-awake now.

I torture him back by grinding my hips and sliding his cock between my thighs.

"Our sex was so good last night that I thought we'd celebrate by having more sex this morning," I breathe out.

His hand slides down my waist straight to my clit, and that's the next place he teases me. I rise up to grab his thick erection and slowly sink down on it.

We both gasp.

Sex with Hudson seems to always get better.

The whole it gets boring with time theory has yet to be proven in our bedroom.

"That's it, ride that cock," he mutters, his eyes shutting.

I shift my hips, rolling them in a circle so I can feel every inch of him.

Then it happens.

I stop at the sound of the doorbell ringing.

And ringing. And ringing.

Then there's a bang on the door.

My phone starts ringing.

His phone starts ringing.

"Ignore it," I plead, dropping my hands down to rest on his chest and rotating my hips into a circle. His groan convinces me he's obliging, but instead, he grips my waist and stops me.

"You riding my cock is the last thing I want to interrupt, but they're blowing our shit up." He starts to get up after I slowly climb off him with a murderous look on my face. "You stay here. I'll get it."

I stop him before he makes it out of bed and point at his lap. "You have an erection the size of the Eiffel Tower. I better get this."

He looks down at his cock that's coated with my juices. *"Fuck,* I promise I'll make it up to you."

I pull on my robe and head downstairs, cursing the air and the person interrupting. Willow rushes in barefoot when I throw the door open. Her hair looks like a rat's nest. Her dress is wrinkled, and her makeup looks like she got into a fight with the sprinkler.

"What the hell?" I mutter. "Where have you been?"

Last night was a blur to me—thanks to all of the celebratory alcohol we drank after getting home and the mind-blowing sex that followed. I gave Willow a key, so I figured she slipped in quietly and went to bed after leaving the bar with Lauren.

"You look like hell," I continue.

Way to bring a girl down, Stella.

"It doesn't matter," she cries out. "All that matters is I need to leave right fucking now. Can you take me to the airport?"

I follow her as she dashes up the stairs to the guest bedroom.

She drags her suitcase from the closet and starts throwing all her shit inside. "I can take a cab if it'll take you a while. I need to get out of this fucking town as soon as fucking possible."

I grab her arm, turning her around to look at me. "What is going on? What happened?" *Who do I need to kill?*

"I need to go home! That's all you need to know."

"What. Is. Going. On? Did something happen to you last night?"

My stomach sinks.

Did someone hurt her? Was I choosing dick over my best friend's safety?

She sniffles, wiping away the tears. "Do you promise not to tell anyone?"

"It depends on if I need it as justification for murder."

"I slept with Dallas last night."

Whoa. I stumble back.

"What?" I slap myself on the forehead a few times to wake myself up if I'm dreaming.

She didn't just say what I think she did, did she?

"I slept with a man who lost his wife only six months ago. I can't even imagine how much he regrets it." She pauses and holds her finger up. "Wait, I can because he woke up and freaked out when he found me sleeping in his bed."

"Holy shit sticks."

"Tell me about it. I can't face him again. I can't move here. I promise I'll do all of your work from LA. If you need someone closer, you'll have to replace me."

As badly as I want to tell her I'll never be able to replace her, I can't think about work right now. My priority is my best friend.

I run my hand down her hair and pat her shoulder. "It's cool. I get it. We'll figure something out."

"Thank you," she chokes out.

"Let me get dressed, and then I'll take you to the airport."

She nods, and I kiss her on the cheek before leaving the room. My heart is hurting for her.

Hudson is out of bed, his erection gone, and tugging on a shirt when I walk back into the bedroom.

"What's going on?" he asks. "I heard Willow crying but wasn't sure it was my place to go out there."

I shut the door behind me and lower my voice. "Uh … I don't know if I should say."

He stops mid-zipping his jeans. "Is it something serious?"

"Dallas, uh …"

"Dallas?" He grimaces. "Dallas what?"

I'm still trying to find the right words. I have to tell him. As much as I don't want to break my word with Willow, Hudson will find out anyway.

"They slept together last night." The words come out in a rush of breath.

"You're fucking shitting me?"

"I wish I was," I whisper. "She's freaking out. I need to take her to the airport."

"Fuck!" he hisses. "Shit is about to hit the fan."

I shrug. "Maybe it's not such a bad thing. Neither one of them is in a relationship. There's no reason they can't chalk this up as a one-night stand."

"It is a bad thing. Dallas will never forgive himself for this. He had to have been drunk."

"I'm sure Willow was as well … or that it was a mutual attraction. She's not one to date-rape men." If he's trying to insinuate that Willow took advantage of Dallas, we're about to have an argument.

"Hell, that's not what I meant by that, I swear. What I meant was he's probably beating himself up over it right now."

"Go talk to him. See what he's thinking."

He kisses me. "Be careful. Call me when you're on your way back home from the airport."

CHAPTER FORTY-TWO

Hudson

DALLAS IS SITTING in his living room when I walk in. A bottle of whiskey hangs from his fingers. His face is drowning in regret—his eyes red-rimmed and glossy.

We stare at each other for a moment before I move farther into the room and take the seat on the other side of the sectional. I stopped in the guest room to see Willow before I left my house. I wanted to tell her goodbye and assure her that I'll talk to him. She looked like a hot mess, and I have no doubt they're both struggling with this.

"Where's Maven?" is my first question. Not only can we not have this discussion if she's here but he also can't be drinking like this around her. "I can have Stella come get her for a while."

He shakes his head. "She spent the night at Mom and Dad's." His voice shakes. "You know, don't you?"

I rub my hand over my face when he takes a drink. "Do I know that Willow just fled our house like there's a plague outbreak here because something happened between the two of you last night?"

"I feel like the biggest piece of shit in the world, Hudson." His voice cracks. "It's only been months since I lost Lucy. She was my life. *My fucking life.* How could I touch another woman like that? How could I fuck someone else?"

I pause as a brief silence falls between us while struggling to come up with the right words that he won't take the wrong way.

"Eventually …" I stop and take a deep breath. "Sooner or later, you're going to have to move on, brother."

Was that the best thing to say? I don't want him to feel bad about touching Willow. He did nothing wrong.

"Not that fast!" he yells. "I was hers for over a decade! You can't throw that away in six months. *Fuck!* Everyone in this town is going to hate me."

"No one is going to hate you for moving on."

He snorts, the bottle going back to his lips.

"Do you like Willow?"

He stares down at the floor. "Nuh-uh, don't you dare start that shit. I'm not dating anyone for a long ass time. Dating isn't what I need. It sure as hell isn't what Maven needs."

"You're going to stay single and celibate for the rest of your life?"

He looks back up at me. "I haven't decided that yet." He gestures to the house. "I brought her in here. I took her to our bed. Jesus Christ." He throws his arms out in frustration. "I don't know what I'm going to do."

"You're going to be a strong man for your daughter, that's what you're going to do, you hear me? Don't beat yourself up over this. If it was a onetime thing, then so be it. If you like Willow and want to explore shit with her, go for it. It's your choice, and no one is going to look down on you for your decision. There's been plenty of women who've approached me about trying to get close to you, so they have no right to judge for something they're trying to participate in."

"I don't even want to talk about this right now. I feel like complete shit."

I grab the bottle from him. "This isn't going to help."

He frowns. "You suck."

"You need to call Willow."

His skin bunches around his eyes. "And say what? Sorry I freaked out when I woke up and saw you in my bed? There's no way she doesn't hate me right now."

I point the bottle at him. "Make shit right. Stella will kick my ass if Willow quits."

"YOU TALK TO HIM?" Stella asks.

"Yeah. He looks like shit, feels like shit, and doesn't know what to do," I answer.

"You might want to explain to him that you don't talk about how big of a mistake sleeping with someone is *in front of them.* I almost had Willow convinced to move here. There's no changing her mind now. She said I could either hire someone else or let her work from LA." She plops down on our bed. "Everything was going so well. We're building a house. I just got my dream show, and I need my assistant here, not states away. Not to mention, I want to be there for her. She's gone through too much this year with men."

"We'll deal with whatever happens, okay?" I sit down and wrap her in my arms. "You can always visit Willow in LA until she feels comfortable coming here again. We got this."

CHAPTER FORTY-THREE

Hudson

Two Months Later

HER SHINY, ink-black hair lays in a tangle on the pillowcase, and I prop myself up with my elbow to watch her with sleepy eyes.

It's what I do every morning. I wake up and admire the woman in my bed, wondering how I managed to get so damn lucky to have her.

It's not considered creepy doing that, is it?

It's okay if the person you're watching is who you're in love with, right?

I can see that being a stalker's justification, so yes, I guess it is creepy, but I'm not sneaking into her house and watching her sleep.

I'm watching the woman I'm proposing to next month.

I never imagined I'd be here.

I came back to the States devastated after losing the woman I thought I'd spend the rest of my life with. That heartache brought me to the woman who actually deserved my heart and that title. Cameron shitting on me made me realize that no matter what obstacles are thrown my way, or how many miles separate us, my heart will always belong to Stella. I hate the lame-ass cliché—but everything does happen for a reason.

When I took the job with Stella, I thought I was hitting my rock bottom, but I was really smacking face-first into the foundation of who I was and what I wanted. I opened my mind, opened my heart, and moved outside of my small-town boy marrying the small-town girl plan.

Did I think that'd lead me to falling in love with a TV star?

Fuck no.

But hey, shit happens.

Construction has started on our new home on the property I bought from my parents, and Stella decided to keep her house in LA. We travel back and forth when she has promotional events or if we're in need of a quick getaway. I've come to realize that you can make a home anywhere when you're with the one you love.

They've started filming her new show, which results to her being gone as long as fifteen hours a day. Since it's not too far out of town, I get to bring her dinner and watch her work sometimes.

It's one of my favorite parts of my day.

My lips curve up when her eyes shutter open and then narrow my way.

She yawns. "I told you I hate it when you watch me sleep."

I smirk. "It makes my day to know I can be put through anything and no matter what, I still come home to something so damn beautiful. I let you have my side of the closet. Let me enjoy my few seconds of staring without you making a fuss."

She rolls her eyes. "That sounds even creepier." She yawns again. "You all packed?"

I nod, and she snuggles into me, whining.

"I'm going to miss you."

I kiss the top of her head and drag myself out of bed. "I'm going to miss you more."

"I just don't want them to start again," she whispers, concern etched on her face.

"I haven't had them in months, Hollywood. If they do, I'll call you."

I've only had a few flashbacks and nightmares since we've been back together, and those are when she's working late or out of town. Stella is the light to my darkness.

She pouts her lips. "You promise?"

"Promise. I think this retreat will not only help others but it'll benefit me as well."

"I'm so proud of you for making it happen. You're such a sexy badass."

I got some of the guys in my old battalion together, and we started a group that helps soldiers dealing with PTSD. Our first retreat is this weekend in North Carolina, close to where most of us trained. I've been busting my ass this past month to ensure everything will be perfect.

Stella licks her lips when I grab my clothes. "Is it weird how much seeing you naked turns me on?"

"Just as weird as it is me watching you sleep."

"Good thing we found each other." She wiggles around in the sheets and pats the space next to her. "Surely, us creeps have a few minutes to say goodbye to each other properly?"

"You know damn well it'll last more than a few minutes, and as much as I'd love to get some morning sex, I can't. Dallas will be here in about ten minutes." My dick twitches as I pull on my boxer briefs and grab my jeans. "You had me up all night, woman. Your stamina is unbelievable."

Even though Dallas isn't a Marine, he helped me plan this, so I wanted him to be there.

She laughs. "I had to get three days' worth of sex in." Her head tilts to the side when something hits her. "Why is Dallas on his way here? I thought we were picking him up, and then I was dropping you guys off because he didn't want to leave his truck at the airport?"

"Change of plans," I say, not looking at her.

"And that change is?" she asks suspiciously.

"Dallas had to pull out because Maven is sick."

"What?" she screeches. "I told her Dallas would be gone. That was the only way I could convince Willow to come to town this weekend. She's going to think I lied."

"It'll be okay."

She scoffs. "You better say goodbye to me now because it won't be okay. She's going to murder me if she has to face your brother."

"She probably won't even see him. If she does, tell her shit changed at the last minute."

"I'll fly out there."

I've never brought up Willow to Dallas since that morning. It's a she-who-shall-not-be-named situation.

I grab my duffel bag. "I'll text you when I get there, and we'll FaceTime before bed."

She raises a brow. "Are you okay with that?"

"Why wouldn't I be?" We have a nightly ritual where if one of us is going to bed before the other is home, or we're out of town, we FaceTime so we can tell each other good night. It's cheesy, I know, but I fucking love it.

"You're going to be in a cabin with twenty other men."

"And?" I walk back to the bed where she's sitting up on her knees and swipe her tangled hair from her face. "I don't care who's around. I'll always take your call."

She blushes, her lips tilting up in the corners. "I love you, Hudson Barnes. More than you can ever imagine."

I touch my mouth to hers. "I love you, Stella Mendes. The best thing that's ever happened to me."

I kiss her one last time before pulling away. She smacks my ass, laughing, and tells me to have fun.

My nightmares are gone.
My dreams are real.
Stella Mendes is mine.
I'm hers.
My life couldn't get any fucking better.

KEEP UP WITH THE BLUE BEECH SERIES

All books can be read as standalones

Just A Fling
(Hudson and Stella's story)
Just One Night
(Dallas and Willow's story)
Just Exes
(Gage and Lauren's story)
Just Neighbors
(Kyle and Chloe's story)
Just Roommates
(Maliki and Sierra's story)
Just Friends
(Rex and Carolina's story)

ALSO BY CHARITY FERRELL

BLUE BEECH SERIES

(each book can be read as a standalone)

Just A Fling

Just One Night

Just Exes

Just Neighbors

Just Roommates

Just Friends

TWISTED FOX SERIES

Stirred

Shaken

Straight Up

Chaser

Last Round

STANDALONES

Bad For You

Beneath Our Faults

Pop Rock

Pretty and Reckless

Revive Me

Wild Thoughts

RISKY DUET

Risky

Worth The Risk

ABOUT THE AUTHOR

Charity Ferrell resides in Indianapolis, Indiana with her future hubby and two fur babies. She loves writing about broken people finding love with a dash of humor and heartbreak, and angst is her happy place.

When she's not writing, she's making a Starbucks run, shopping online, or spending time with her family.

www.charityferrell.com

CPSIA information can be obtained
at www.ICGtesting.com
Printed in the USA
LVHW090957230921
698554LV00004B/155

9 781672 509237